Silver Heart

Madaline Clifton

Ukiyoto Publishing

DEDICATION

This is a novella dedicated to plenty of people, ranging from my siblings to a pen pal writer friend of mine, per say. Originally meant to be a full length novel, the warmth of the two characters I had fun writing wore off. This is also dedicated to anyone choosing not to give up on their path even when they feel like it. Your voice matters, your words matter.

I'd like to acknowledge those with a deep burning desire for redheads, y'all are as insane as those same redheads! On a more serious note, I'd like to acknowledge those who are brave enough to read something I write. I hope you'll understand it because on a good day, I can't understand my own creations. Y'all are amazing so stay safe, wild, and creative!

Thank you.

Contents

One

The warmth of his tanned hand, brushed her ribcage making her heart flutter causing her to immediately grind her teeth. Her jaw was set as her shamrock green eyes narrowed on the five foot ten, slim and lean, blue eyed man in front of her. She wasn't easily agitated—mind you, but there was something about Sage Landry that pushed her buttons. She swats at his tanned hand while still scowling at the warmth he caused to pass between them. "Can you watch where you're touching, sir?"

"Ma'am, you're in my way, remember?" Sage gently mused, scanning the green eyes of Cat Devereaux. His hair was short, full of chestnut brown curls. He was smitten with blue denim as a half smile appeared on his full, dark pink lips upon Cat tensing. He towered over the twenty nine year old who caught his attention from the moment she returned to the Devereaux Ranch.

Cat's breath rose and fell, keeping a steady gaze on the twenty one year old in her view. She was five foot two, petite with olive skin, and dark pink lips. Her thick, dark brown, shoulder length curls bounced as she shook her head at the young man. She had recently returned home to Silver Hart, Montana after things didn't pan out for her. "I'm not in your way, Sage. Can you please move out of my way?"

Sage lifted a hand to caress her chin, tilting her head upwards. His face inched closer to hers, brushing his lips gently to hers all the while watching her shudder. He knew what they had between them and what she chose to dance around, wondering if Cat would always maintain the distance between them. "Cat, you can't ignore the spark long ignited between us."

"I'm not ignoring anything, Sage. There's nothing between us—there never has been and never will be. Got it?" Cat scoffed, utterly confused about what Sage was speaking into existence. She knew they shared a type of chemistry that could be chalked up to one word: *lust*, but that was it.

Sage blew a breath, dropping his hand from her face; slaying the warmth they shared. His deep blue eyes wandered her body as sadness clutched his heart. "I'm sorry, ma'am. I'll be getting back to attending the Ranch. You take care."

Cat watched the broad shouldered man wander off causing her to blow a sigh of relief. She heard the front door of the three bedroomed, two bathroom, cobblestone Ranch house slam shut with conviction. She placed a hand over her heart while placing the other hand on top of the fireplace as the black cowboy boots she wore gave her some height. The off-shoulder, mid-thigh light orange dress she wore, nearly proved too much. Before she could speak, the front door once again creaked open and voices floated from the entrance of the house towards the living room.

"You will be happy to stay." Tasmin Devereaux was assuring the person she was with. She was a fair skinned, five foot eleven, slim but curvy woman. Her eyes were sea green with freckles galore and long flowing, strawberry brunette waves. She was in an off-shoulder purple, snug fitting shirt with a brown skirt that maintained a slit in the right side.

Her boots were a dark brown—a set of cowboy boots just like Cat. She was thirty two and the oldest of the Devereaux sisters. She was speaking to a hushed yet nervous person which gripped Cat.

Cat pushed herself up with the help of the mantle before striding towards the entrance of the living room. Her heart slowed, thumped in her chest, died then revived with a soft flutter upon the six foot one, lean and lanky porcelain male accompanying her older sister. "We have company?"

He wasn't just any male. He was a thirty one year old with short, fiery ginger curls stripping Cat of the oxygen in her lungs. His eyes were an icy pale green that should have been healing but just irritated Cat to no end. He was also the step-cousin of Cat, Taz, Jade and Tavi. "Catarina."

Cat scowled, folding her arms to her bosom. "Why is he hogging the air we breathe?"

"Don't mind, Cat. She's sour about a few things lately. Her career didn't pan out like she assumed it would." Tasmin murmured, cutting Cat a dead eyed glare.

"We don't need a dead eyed ginger running amuck while we bury our heads in the sand, Taz." Cat sharply bit off, watching the amusement in the icy pale green eyes of October Winston grow. His lips were soft pink, inviting and drawing up memories that she shrugged off. She couldn't think about their days well spent together because it was wrong on so many levels.

"October, I am so sorry for the rudeness of Cat. Truly. I'll show you to your room." Tasmin quickly speaks up, shooting Cat a glare once more as she simply rolls her eyes.

Cat had every right to hold onto her graceful, beautiful, steely resolve. Her and October held eye contact—hardly breaking as the universe shook something in her. She was always shook when October came around which is why she made the habit of disappearing when he turned up. "Why is he staying with us?"

Tasmin held up a finger, shoving October towards the hall, waiting for him to get a move on. She then led him down the hallway to the set of three bedrooms, nodding for him to head to the former bedroom of Jade Devereaux who was living her best life at Silver Hart University. She scurried back towards Cat, half tempted to smack her in the face. "Catarina, what is wrong with you? You cannot talk to family like that, especially not October Winston!"

"I can't help it, Taz. October and I have bad blood for reasons only the two of us should ever know." Cat says, frowning as the memories of the two remained stripped from her mind. She didn't like the magnetic pull the ginger had over her ever since they were teenagers nor did she like it when he walked back through their front door.

"You are going to have to control your anger with him, Cat. He's a possible investor to keep our ranch running—without money, it's hard to maintain this place. He inherited his father's money, don't piss him off." Tasmin informs Cat with her jaw set, allowing her hands to extend towards the shoulder of her middle sister.

Cat searches the sea green eyes of Tasmin, catching the concern in them. "Taz, what's really eating you?"

Tasmin released her grip on Cat, storming off to the outside. She hurried down the dark oak porch of the ranch home, beginning to pace in front of the house. She was beyond worried which struck fear in Cat.

Cat rushed out of the house, following the quickened pace of her older sister. She had no idea just how troubled Tasmin was.

"Our home is in great trouble. We will lose it. I'm just one person and Octavia nor her soon-to-be 'baby daddy' help with the pay." Tasmin squeaked, coming clean to Cat who felt some relief roll off of her sister in waves.

Cat fished in her bra for the money she had saved from her time on the road. How could she have thought she would become a singer let alone a writer? Her dreams were nothing more than a pipe dream. "Taz, I'm heading to the Clock tomorrow, but hopefully this helps unburden you by some amount."

Tasmin's sea green eyes widened as Cat pressed the cash into her palm. She knew it would take loads more to keep their house from being owned by the bank. She knew that Cat and October had some kind of strained relationship, but the more help they got for the Devereaux Ranch; the better. She pulled Cat in for a grateful hug. "Thank you, but you still have to be kind to him."

Cat frowned, cutting her eyes to the ranch house where October remained. Rolling her shamrock green eyes, she considered the wise words of Tasmin. She shuddered upon the hug, quickly pulling out of it. She sighed. "Do you think I'll be able to get my old job back at the Clock?"

"Why don't you make some of your Orange Creme Pie and find out?" Tasmin lightly chuckled, wiping away a few stray tears. She shook her head. "I didn't mean to dump all my financial issues on you, Cat. I'm just stressed."

Cat squeezed the shoulder of her older sister. "I completely understand, Taz. This house and land of fifty acres has been in our family for generations. Have you prompted Sage to pay you since he's staying in the barn?"

A black barn with lavender trim was present— just a brief walk from the house. There was a half moon in silver interconnected with a full sun. No one could ever comprehend what it meant. The barn kept three horses and there were at least two cats stalking about the property.

"He works for us, Cat!" Tasmin hissed, causing Cat to snort.

"You allowed him to turn the barn into a house of sorts, yes?" Cat asked, jutting out her hip as she grew unamused by how easy her sister could be. Her shamrock green eyes bore into the barn as something didn't sit right with her. "If he has running water, electricity, would that not warrant bills? Our ranch isn't too difficult to maintain with three horses, some cattle and a sheep or two."

"Don't forget the two cats that wander aimlessly around." Tasmin muttered causing a grin to split the face of Cat whose eyes held a smirk.

"Blu and Piper are still roaming around?" Cat continued to grin while Tasmin slowly nodded.

Piper was a gray and white female cat with partly yellow orange eyes. Her brother was a black and white tuxedo with the same matching eyes and neurological condition.

Blu and Piper were named and raised by Cat who had to leave them behind when she chose the creative life. Her favorite was Blu who's head had increasingly tilted, further striking worry in her. None of them had ever been able to afford to take the cats, born on the twenty second of May to a vet. "Blubear! Piper!"

Calling for the cats seemed to work as they came rushing up, pursuing one another with a quickness.

Cat felt a blush light up her features once she reached down to play with Blu who loved her more than Piper did. Her blush was due to the reminder of why and how she came up with the name of Blu for the cat. She shuddered, shrugging off the memory. "Taz, you should consider asking for rent from Sage. We should probably all chip in."

Tasmin pressed her hands to her waistline, eyeing the black barn. She grew curious, aware that her sister was right. She cleared her throat. "Want to join me then?"

Cat grinned, jabbing Blu before returning to her height. She followed Tasmin's steely gaze. Since when did she invoke that emotion in her older sister? She had that same cold anger moments ago when October Winston appeared back in her life. "Sure."

Tasmin led the way to the barn with Cat next to her. She frowned as a stench so foul wafted to her nostrils. Did the barn always smell like something rotten and decaying? She gagged, catching the stoic glance of uncertainty rolling off of Cat. "Do barns always smell like death?"

Cat sighed, taking the lead from her sister. She stepped into the barn, further investigating where the smell was coming from, soon, wishing she hadn't. She clammed up, tensing as a small squeak escaped her. "Don't come up!"

Two

Tasmin grew cold and confused, having not moved an inch since her sister called to her not to come up. She ran her hand along the rail of the wood stair as she finally did what Cat told her not to do. She gagged some more as she entered the loft of the barn with horror opening her sea green eyes. She couldn't believe what they were seeing. She shouldn't have allowed Sage Landry to run the Devereaux Ranch. "I...oh my...what the...?!"

Cat was also at a loss for words. She proceeded to open then close her mouth, fishing for what could work. She extended a hand to the gray palomino in the middle of a pentagram—guts on full display, having bled out. "I'm going to have nightmares for the rest of my sensitive life."

Tasmin opened her mouth to utter a smart remark to Cat, but came up blank. The back of her eyelids pricked with tears. She came up with nothing just as a gasp came from behind the two women.

"Ladies, are you alright? You probably shouldn't be here." Sage Landry coughed, gathering their attention.

Tasmin became engulfed with hatred towards their ranch hand. "Do you call sacrificing a horse to your insolent beast work?"

"Whatever possessed you to do this, Landry?" Cat spoke in turn for a shaking Tasmin. She inched closer to her sister, just so Taz didn't feel alone.

Sage chuckled, pacing in front of the two women. "I didn't sacrifice your horses. Someone else wanted your attention with me being the messenger. I quite frankly delivered."

Tasmin stumbled into Cat, grateful for her middle sister. She finally closed her mouth after holding it open in astonishment on behalf of their deceased wildlife. "I have no idea what's going on."

"You wouldn't. Check the Grim which is a purple and orange book with a silver half moon. Your grandfather gave it to you before his lungs were ripped from his chest on Christmas Eve...last year." Sage beautifully explained to the women.

Tasmin pressed her lips into a thin line. She knew the exact book Sage was mentioning yet it was more or less a telegram; not a book. "Grandpa Morris ate that thing, thinking it was a Christmas cookie. You didn't rip his lungs out."

"I didn't say I did. Lucien Redmond hardly kills in cleanliness." Sage said, snapping his fingers before disappearing in a swirl of frostbite. He left the two women cold as could be.

"Lucien Redmond? What kind of twisted name is that?" Cat mindlessly asked, not really needing an answer as her brain processed what her sister said.

"Grandpa Morris died? He was my best friend with a wicked sense of humor and the best advice giver."

October had long got settled, having caught sight of the direction in which Tasmin and Cat wandered off. He followed the two women to the barn—kept warm by his green and black checkered flannel jacket. He cleared his throat. "Tasmin? Catarina?"

Cat jumped at the sound of his deep, concerned voice causing her to snort. "The cavalry has arrived. Why don't you earn your keep, October by burying Grayson—poor horse. I'll get Hunter to help. He's shacked up with Tavi, yeah?"

Tasmin nodded to October who briefly gave Cat a pointed look. "Do as she said, we'll speak later about whatever has been going on without our knowledge. Thank you, Oct."

October lifted one ginger colored eyebrow, tilting his head at Tasmin and Cat; finding their request unbelievable. However, he saw Cat gulp upon brushing past him while shuddering just the same. He knew exactly what it meant. "Sure."

Tasmin hesitated before scurrying after Cat because she barely heard a lick of what either of them were saying. She caught up to Cat who was halfway across the half green, half yellow grass riddled lawn. "Wait, Cat! Wait!"

Cat stopped short, catching sight of the one story, two bedroom cottage house in back—made of black cherry smoked wood. She eyed the meadows, shrouded by trees, hiding the spot a way—just barely. If she hadn't grown up on the Devereaux Ranch she wouldn't have known about the beautiful, cozy, small spacious area. "What?"

Tasmin began to vigorously shake her head at Cat, biting the inside of her cheek. She did not want Cat to interrupt whatever could possibly be happening between Tavi and Hunter. "What if Tavi and Hunter are in the process of trying for a child?"

"Doubtful." Cat muttered before marching directly to the front door of the cottage house. She frowned, taken aback when Hunter Coleman peeled open the door with ease.

Hunter Coleman was six foot one with broad shoulders and a nicely tanned, well sculpted body that any woman could love. His eyes were a light green with a head of short, black hair and a cheeky grin to accompany. He was a lawyer, but answered the door in only a towel. "Yes, sisters of Tavi?"

Tasmin's sea green eyes explored the body of Hunter as if she hadn't ever seen a man in her life. The last guy she had been with did a number on her so badly that she craved forgetting the absurd idea of dating. She shook her head. "Our family seems to enjoy dark haired men a little too well."

Cat begged to differ. There was one guy who always had her striving for more between them. Nor did he have a head full of dark hair causing her to internally groan. "Biased much, sister?"

"I'm not biased, I just...hold the phone..." Tasmin held up a hand to tell Hunter to wait as her eyes pierced Cat. She had known about the crush on a particular person Cat had when they were teenagers, but was unaware of anything further. She did a double take, raising a strawberry brunette eyebrow at Cat.

Cat proceeded to smirk, soon wiggling her eyebrows at Tasmin. "Do you not recall Simon Wheeler? I dated him for about five years before I chose to leave him behind. I was in love—his head was full of light chocolate brown curls; not black curls."

Hunter cleared his throat. "I was getting ready for work, ladies. I don't have all day to listen to stories of your love life even though Tasmin is right. Light chocolate brown hair is still dark; considered brunette, just like you, Catarina."

Cat shuddered in disgust from the use of her full name falling from the lips of Hunter. She hadn't ever liked the man, not exactly hiding the fact. She did shove it down when Tavi Devereaux—the twenty seven year old, third oldest sister proclaimed her love for Hunter. "October Winston, our step-cousin is in the barn—"

"Whoa! October is back? Winter hasn't hit us yet." Hunter spoke up with ease, having taken a liking to October while the second Devereaux sister was out of town. He grinned from ear to ear. "What can I do for you?"

"October is in the barn, burying a horse that Sage Landry chose to sacrifice to the insolent beast that he worships. I knew hiring someone who had a different belief wouldn't work, but Tavi and Jade insisted." Tasmin groaned, answering Hunter before Cat could speak.

Hunter Coleman was a forty year old, having an affair with a younger woman whom he loved. He clasped his hands together as he gestured to his body. "I will get dressed then go help October before heading to work."

As soon as Hunter softly closed the door, Cat angrily turned to Tasmin. "Since when does he know October? He's a forty year old man—"

Tasmin placed a hand over Cat's mouth to shush her. She proceeded to explain what her sister had been missing out on. "October has been visiting us every year. Throughout. On and off. He's had time to get to know Hunter, vice versa."

Cat then rolled her eyes, unable to believe the fact that October came to the Devereaux Ranch every year. She wondered if his home life was fine or if there was more buried underneath the surface of it all. Shrugging, she wiped her hands down to smooth out the wrinkles in her dress.

The front door popped open once more with Hunter in view. He was dressed in a black tuxedo with a red tie and a white button up long sleeve shirt. His shoes were sleek, black, non-slip dress shoes. He made sure to pat a black briefcase he carried, holding it up so the sisters could see it. "I'm ready."

"We also need to see Tavi about a telegram." Cat added, watching the false cheer and enthusiasm on Hunter's face falter. Her dark brown eyebrows rose, watching the man with caution.

"Sure." Hunter agreed in a clear cut, steely voice. He brushed past the two women who were just looking after their sister. He knew they weren't going to be overjoyed with how they found Tavi Devereaux. "Be safe, ladies."

"Don't you dare, Cat!" Tasmin hissed, erasing the doubt that Cat could speak into the air. She quite frankly didn't want to hear it as she entered the dark, stale cottage house.

Cat visibly flinched, wincing as she began to withdraw curtains to kill the staleness of the formerly dark and messy cottage house. She grew anxious, cutting her eyes around when Tavi wasn't seen. "Octavia!"

No noise came from the house stirring panic mode for both of the sisters.

Tasmin began to clean the house but nodded to Cat. "You check her bedroom. If he has so much as harmed her—"

"We will invoke the wrath of the Devereaux ancestors to take him out." Cat agreed, finishing Tasmin's thought out loud. She marched towards the small, thin hall where the bedrooms would be. She burst into the bedroom where a complete mess was.

Tavi Devereaux was a five foot four, olive skinned, petite woman. Her long flowing, charcoal brown hair was a mess as she sat on the edge of her bed with her face pressed into her legs. Her navy green eyes were red rimmed, puffy from all the crying the woman covered in blood had been doing. She sniffles, having tuned out the real world for far too long.

Cat was going to eradicate Hunter Coleman when he returned. She saw the sight of Tavi Devereaux as she rushed over, inspecting the twenty seven year old from head to toe. "TASMIN!"

The roar in Cat's voice made Tasmin drop dirty plates that she had begun to scrub. She heard the clatter, thud, and shatter but that did not matter. She rushed up the stairs upon hearing the anger and quiver in the tone of Cat. "What did he do to her?"

Tavi could barely make out their voices, but the question was one she asked herself on a daily basis. The ringing in her ears subsided. "I did this to myself when I agreed to be his. The blood isn't from him, but from the several miscarriages I have been producing."

Cat noted dry blood—new and old with the smell of death rolling off of Tavi. It had been painfully obvious when she first saw her sister. She grunts as she forces Tavi to get up, aided by Tasmin. "We need to get her out of here and to the hospital!"

Tasmin worked to take more of Tavi's weight from Cat who didn't utter another word. She helped Cat get Tavi down stairs, just barely out the door of the cottage house when October saw them from the distance, grew concerned, and rushed their way.

"What the Hell?" October asked, eyeing Tasmin who couldn't find her words and a steely Cat. He picked Tavi up, grunting as he let Tasmin and Cat lead the way so they could get their sister healed.

Three

"We have no choice, but to leave her at Silver Hart Memorial." Cat reassured Tasmin who sighed, nodding in agreement.

"I know." Tasmin voiced, chewing on the inside of her cheek. She thought they should check out *The Grim* while Tavi Devereaux got the care she needed.

October had been with them, volunteered by Cat to stay and keep watch over Tavi. He was happy to do it, but not when he was volunteered on the behalf of the impulsive Cat Devereaux. He swallowed, sitting with the third oldest Devereaux sister while Tasmin informed him about the Grim.

Cat cut her eyes to October over her shoulder long enough for his icy pale green ones to make contact. A light, brief blush coated her cheeks causing her to shoot it down. "If The Grim is a telegram, can't we just open it here?"

"No. You two should probably go and check it out while I stay with Octavia." October softly replied, not wanting to scare the hospitalized woman. He was wrong to befriend Hunter Coleman, thinking he was a great guy. He could imagine if it was the one he adored laying in the bed. "Call me, if you find anything out."

Cat heard the softness in the depths of October's voice, wanting to respond. By the time a response came, her mind had tossed it out the door causing a drought of forgetfulness to kick in. "We will."

Tasmin was the first one to exit Silver Hart Memorial, creeped out by the hospital. She waited for Cat to slide into the dark purple convertible she owned before cruising out of the hospital parking lot. "Grandpa Morris knew about The Grim which is why we should search his things at home."

"Good idea, but what exactly are we looking for when we find it?" Cat asks, raising an eyebrow.

Tasmin scoffed. "I'm not entirely sure, but it's a purple and orange book with a silver half moon. Sage already voiced as much."

"Sage is an ignoramus." Cat rolled her shamrock green eyes, shaking her chocolate curls. An idea slid into her mind. "What about Tavi's house? What about Hunter Coleman? What do we do about that jerk off?"

"We can figure it out whenever we stumble across The Grim. The Grim might even be able to help us ward off Hunter." Tasmin spoke, tapping her fingers on the steering wheel. She worked her jawline with her mind working overtime. "I cannot believe magic exists, can you?"

"Um, it's always existed. It's nothing new. Where were you when I was attending Silver Hart

High?" Cat did a double take, eyeing Tasmin upon tilting her head towards her sister.

Tasmin hadn't attended Silver Hart High. She recalled her mother shipping her off to boarding school for the gifted, but nothing came of it. She eventually returned home with a less than thrilled attitude with the deed of the house, land, and such being passed down not just to her but her sisters as well. She sighed. "I was shipped off to boarding school, remember?"

Cat frowned, processing the information of Tasmin. She couldn't believe she didn't remember where her sister was when she was sixteen. Of course, she had been all too wrapped up in red at the time. She sighed. "I must have been overly busy with my personal life at the time, Taz. I'm sorry for not noticing or being a better sister."

"Catarina, you have nothing to apologize for. You were sixteen, living your best life. I'm three years older than you—it's to be expected." Tasmin gently spoke, reaching to squeeze the shoulder of Cat in a show of reassurance.

Cat felt far from reassured as she sighed, trying to recall the events of her past. In doing so, she had a blank space only to catch the beautiful blues of the mountains in the distance. She was smitten with the fresh, cool air brushing against her skin, reviving the hope buried in her heart. "I should remember my childhood, Taz."

"We all should, but who really does?" Tasmin chuckled, finally pulling up to the Devereaux Ranch house with an eeriness taking root. She was the first one to exit the vehicle, slowly taking steps towards her home.

Slamming the door of the purple convertible saw Tasmin visibly flinch as Cat stepped up beside her, half smirking. "Sorry about the slam of the door. I didn't think it'd go that hard. So, we have some of Grandpa's stuff here?"

"Yep. Follow me." Tasmin said, leading the way into their house. She shivered at how quiet and chilly the cobblestone house appeared. She knew she would have to put on a fire in order to attempt to heat the house to keep them warm. Her family didn't have a central heat unit to keep them warm during the colder weather in Silver Hart.

Cat followed Tasmin into the living room with a flat screen television clinging to the wall, the window to the right with curtains dangling down, the glass coffee table with the worn down, cozy, light gray sofa in front of it. She smiled at the place, running her fingers down her dress. "I really miss Grandpa Morris. How come you didn't send word that he died? He was my favorite person."

Tasmin groaned as she pulled a box from next to the television hanging on the wall via the floor. She had strode to the right side, fidgeting in the corner before she held the small, rectangular box up to Cat's view. "I didn't tell you, Cat, because up until Sage—I wasn't even aware of his death. Thank you."

Cat pouted, folding her arms to her bosom as Tasmin plucked the top from the box, digging around for The Grim. She softly rubbed at her eyelids once Tasmin retrieved a purple and orange book with a silver half moon. Of course, she thought the thing looked more like a tablet, of sorts. "Looks like a silver tablet, Taz."

Tasmin proceeded to nod her head, lightly touching a finger to the top of the telegram. "Yes, it would appear as a tablet since it's a telegram."

Cat waited for something to happen while Tasmin fumbled with the telegram. She gasped when a glimmer of blue engulfed the tablet, bringing to life a hologram version of Grandpa Morris. She harshly gulped, frowning at how little it had in comparison with her flesh and blood grandfather. "Grandpa Morris?"

"Dear Granddaughters, if you have discovered the telegram then the truth will be invoked into you. With great Fae Magic, comes disastrous responsibility. I hope you're prepared." The man hoarsely spoke before touching a hand to Tasmin before vanishing directly into her via her forehead.

Cat sucked in a sharp air of breath as the wind seemed to flee from her lungs. A wave of energy sent shivers coursing through her body as a brief gleam of light touched her. She cleared her throat, cutting her shamrock green eyes to a stunned Tasmin. "What in the world? We didn't get answers!"

"For a change, you're right, Cat. We got left with more questions than anything. If Sage was after a telegram then he won't find it." Tasmin mutters, shaking her head of wavy strawberry brown hair.

Cat would figure out of all the people who had answers then it would be her big sister or her grandpa. She sighed. "We have nothing. Where do we go from here, Taz?"

Tasmin nonchalantly shrugged, thinking about the cottage house. "I think we should get to work cleaning up the cottage house. I don't know how we're going to keep Hunter from returning to our property."

Cat nodded in agreement with her sister. "Fine, but why don't you clean it up since you obsess over that type of stuff? I have a different approach I could take."

"What's your different approach, Catarina?" Tasmin inquired, eyeing her sister from head to toe.

Cat smiled. "I could stop in town and find out if anyone knows anything."

"About Fae Magic?" Tasmin half squeaked, shaking her head in disagreement. She touched a hand to her forehead, mentally confirming that Cat had flipped a lid. "No."

"Yes." Cat disagreed, sheepishly smiling as she started for the road. She couldn't drive then, she wouldn't drive now. She saw the horror in the sea green eyes of Tasmin. "Relax, Taz, I know exactly what I'm doing. I do know somebody who might know something. Our friendship is as stale and old as time."

"Wh-who?" Tasmin squeaks, feeling the color leave her face. She caught the ever-growing smirk on the face of her middle sister.

"Simon Wheeler." Cat spoke the name into existence with a sour aftertaste, brewing in her mouth. She knew the thirty one year old would be more than likely to reject helping her. She had ripped his heart into tiny shreds, dancing on it by accident.

"That's a highly bad idea. Didn't you two date?" Tasmin softly mused while searching her brain for the brief encounter she had of the couple. She had been home for the holidays and they seemed like they were in love. She would assume if Cat and Simon had been a thing to the present date then Cat wouldn't have left him so willingly.

Cat really didn't fancy the idea of meeting up with her ex-boyfriend. She thought he might be helpful in this situation plus she fancied seeing if the man still looked as good as he did when they dated. She shouldn't have let anyone talk her into getting wasted, because when she did—she spilled secrets to Simon that killed everything they had. "Taz, that's also true, but I know what I'm doing."

"I'll trust you, because you're my sister, Catarina. I don't actually trust that your ex-boyfriend will be so willing to work with you." Tasmin called, remembering the forest green eyes of Simon Wheeler. She saw him everyday when she stopped by the Swift Rose.

Cat was sure Simon had the same pale skin with broad shoulders, slender and lanky body as well as his short, light chocolate brown curls. She was also sure that his soft pink, kissable lips hadn't changed. Why would they? Grunting, she waved at Tasmin before beginning her lengthy trek into the heart of the town. It took her a good bit to reach the Swift Rose— a small, wooden, silver and red pub with a thin audience; most people in Silver Hart were too busy working to stop for liquor. She shuddered as eyes pierced the entire journey from the barn to the pub, aware that it was more than likely Sage, keeping tabs on her.

Simon Wheeler was five foot nine, wiping down the bar of the pub upon Cat Devereaux entering the front, wooden, slightly oval door. He didn't look up right away, but his younger half brother coughed to gather his attention. He rolled his forest green eyes when they landed on the brunette woman. "Catherine, what are you doing here?"

Cat winced. "Catarina is my full name. How can you not remember?"

"Coming from the one who couldn't bother to remember my middle name let alone my birthday. I don't know how I could forget." Simon's voice was laced with venom towards Cat who broke him. If he could wrap his hands around her throat to watch the light dim then he would. He pointed towards the front door. "Get out and don't come back!"

Cat felt the sting of pain she had caused Simon as sorrow clutched her heart. She hadn't meant to hurt him, then again, what happened isn't what she meant to transpire in the first place. "Si, I'm sorry."

Four

Theodore Wheeler was twenty seven with broad shoulders, fair skin, standing at five foot nine inches in height. His opal eyes burned into the side of Cat Devereaux becoming saddened. He briefly ran a hand through his short, coffee brown curls. He was dressed in a red and black checkered flannel jacket over a light gray tee shirt, showing the muscle he bore. His pants were black as he snapped his fingers at Cat.

"Cat?" Theo inquired, causing Cat to slowly look his way.

"Theo?" Cat asked in turn, watching a small smile slip onto his lips. She felt some relief stir in her heart. "What's up?"

"You seem to have made a friend. To your right, in the corner." Theo nodded to a guy who resembled Sage Landry.

Coldness surged to life within Cat who cracked her knuckles about to start a pub fight. "Thank you, Theo, but you may want to call an ambulance."

Theo scoffed. "Why?"

Instead of answering, Cat approached the five foot ten, lean and lanky male who may have shared a similar appearance to Sage, but it wasn't Sage. She noted the darker shade of short, brown curls with silver blue eyes once the twenty one year old met her gaze. She raised one eyebrow, nodding to the young man sitting in the corner as if waiting. "Who are you? Why do you look like Sage Landry?"

"I..." The younger man opened his mouth, proceeding to trail off. He was waiting for her to take a seat before he bothered to go into a further explanation. "Take a seat or you'll leave the same way you came in—clueless."

Cat sighed, slowly plopping down across from the man. She didn't have anywhere else to be causing her to work her jawline. "Who are you? What do you know?"

He finally met her gaze with such hostility it was like being stung by a fire ant. His nostrils were flaring since his life had been ruined by the clone, built from his image, stolen from his last name. "I'm Gem Landry. Sage Landry is a clone, built from my image, stolen from my last name."

"What does Sage want with a telegram that belonged to our Grandpa Morris?" Cat inquired, watching the wheels turn in the silver blue eyes of Gem Landry. She couldn't believe a word of what he was saying. Why was he so eager to share such information with her? She was thinking that if he was so good that he would gift her such information.

Leaning into Cat, Gem searched her eyes, placing his hands on either of her wrists. "Tell me, you still have the telegram."

"Tasmin and I found the telegram. She touched it, a blue glow happened, we saw a brief hologram of our grandpa then he disappeared into Taz." Cat inhaled sharply as relief flourished in his silver blue eyes. She wasn't a touchy person yet she didn't refuse Gem touching her, feeling no type of way about it.

"This is good news. This means you and your sisters have been given your Fae Magic back. You had them in your teen years, but your parents opted for a cruel fate until adulthood." Gem said, lightly rubbing a thumb over the back of one of her hands. His knees were shaking under the table as his eyes searched hers once more.

Cat was under the impression that Gem was anxious, given his mixed reaction to things. "How do you know about any of it?"

"I am the guardian of Jade Devereaux. We're the same age. I'm what you call an Air Shifter. You'll come to learn about my kind in time, but for now—focus on self discovery." Gem muttered, truly freaking Cat out.

Scowling, Cat quickly removed her hands from underneath Gem. She slid from the booth, stopping short when a familiar figure came into view. She saw him stride up to the pub, having an idle chat with Simon. Her hands rested on her waistline. Should she scare the dick out of October or leave him to converse with her ex-boyfriend?

Sharp pain shot through the heart of Cat causing her shamrock green eyes to become misty. She would have approached October, but what would be the point? She turned around in order to eye the door of the pub as Gem got to his feet. "I have to get out of here."

"I'll join you." Gem mumbled, sliding from the booth, taking note of the color leaving her face. He placed a hand around her shoulders, shielding Cat from the view of October and Simon while Theo watched on in evident amusement.

Cat usually would shrug off the arm of another, but was too stunned about seeing October who should have been watching over Tavi. She wondered if something happened. "H-How do you know my sister?"

Gem lightly chuckled, keeping an arm around Cat, rubbing soothing circles into her right shoulder. He sighed. "I told you, Catarina, in due time; you'll learn about my kind. Just go home and look after your sisters."

Cat caught the smirk blooming on his face causing her to snort. "Sage Landry is a stalker who sacrificed our horses to this insolent beast. Do you know anything else that could help us?"

A knowing gleam appeared in his silver blue eyes. He nonchalantly shrugged, dropping his hand from around her shoulders once they walked a good distance. "I don't."

Cat could tell that Gem was lying, creating a new irritation under her skin. She rolled her shamrock green eyes at him. "Guys love to lie, especially to the women in their lives. Have y'all no shame?"

Gem lightly touched her bottom lip before taking a few more strides back from Cat. "In due time, Cat."

"Why are you saying my name like that?" Cat asked, shuddering due to goosebumps that clung to her skin. She would need to change when she walked through the front door of the house. She saw Gem vanish, becoming one with the wind, making her wonder. She shook her head, not believing it possible as she returned home.

"Cat?" Tavi Devereaux weakly mumbled once Cat appeared, stopping in the doorway of the living room. She looked healthier, less dead as she shot her second older sister a smile. "Is October with you? He went looking for you."

"Didn't look like the ginger devil was looking for me." Cat irritably voiced, having left before the ginger could force her into the same space as him. She should have known that's why he turned up. Of all the people that were good at finding her even in the darkest of places, October Winston always stumbled across her and it got on her nerves. She needed alone time just like any normal human being.

"Ginger devil? Good one. Your quips are still strong." Tavi grinned, equally as wicked with a mean streak when it came to personality only to match with Cat. She had a black blanket with faux fur placed on her lap, patting the spot on the sofa next to her; pining for Cat to join her. Her charcoal brown hair remained a mess of dried, dirty sweat, but her body was cleansed.

Cat slowly walked over, sitting down beside Tavi. "I need to shower, dry off and change out of this torture. I feel like I've been giving off the wrong impressions all day."

"Nonsense, KitCat." Tavi touched a hand to Cat's arm as she shook her head. She had a cold sweat while she did what she could to reassure Cat about her appearance. "You look darling."

Sadness swept through Cat at the miserable state of Octavia Devereaux. She did the one thing she did for no one outside of those she cared about. She wrapped her arms around Tavi, pulling her sister into a lengthy, very much needed embrace. "I love you, Tavi."

Tavi's breath hitched in her throat as the reminder of what she had been through resurfaced in her mind. She weakly sighed as she sobbed into the chest of Cat. She hated herself for allowing someone like Hunter Coleman to fool her into believing she had to stay locked away in order to build a family. She was certain she wouldn't ever trust anyone ever again after the older man. "I can't believe I was a fool to believe..."

"Okay, Satine...let's not play the blame game. You were in love, you loved him. He gave you nothing, stripping you of yourself." Cat half smirked at the reference she was sure Tavi understood. She began to massage soothing circles in the back of her sister in hopes to comfort and reassure the twenty seven year old.

"I hate myself." Tavi breathed into Cat but the more she sobbed, the more her eyes dried. She noted a glow of orange coming from her sister, believing it to be nothing more than hope blossoming within. She began to instantly feel better knowing she had sisters she could count on. "I can't stay in the cottage house, not with Hunter lurking wherever he chooses."

"You can stay in my room with me. This way, you aren't by yourself and he can't harass you without facing one of your sisters' wrath." Cat gently mumbled, becoming relieved upon Tavi overflowing with hope.

The front door banged open as an irritated seeming October Winston appeared in the doorway of the living room. His nostrils were flaring, just barely calming down when his eyes set on Cat and Tavi. "Catarina, what is your problem? Taz asked me to get you once Tavi bounced back. How could you lose me once you realized I was onto you?"

Refraining from the pet name on the tip of her tongue, she rolled her green eyes. She found his anger amusing as she shrugged. "I didn't lose you, October. I didn't even know you were stalking me. I was getting information that failed to provide any real nugget."

Tavi lightly nudged the shoulder of Cat. "Give him a break. He's looking out for you and he's a possible investor for the ranch in order to save us until we can bring in more money on our own. Be a little nicer."

"You are starting to sound like Taz. You're both wrong. I don't have to be nice to the ginger tailed reindeer." Cat yawned, waving at the seething redhead. She saw his blood pressure rise some more, but how he felt wasn't her problem.

October shook his head at Cat. "Why can't you ever be nice to me, Catarina? I've done nothing wrong to you—then or now."

Those words chilled Cat to the very bone. She took those words with implications to their past a bit too personally. She had been nice to October when they were teenagers, in doing so, they both ruined their lives. And, for what? Disgust brewed in the pit of her stomach as she stood up from her spot on the sofa. She cut the redhead an icy, angry glare that diminished his own as she approached him. "I was nice to you and look where it got me."

October frowned, not sure what to say to those words. "Catarina, I—"

"You shouldn't use my full name. You don't know me like you think you do." Cat bit off with fresh hurt in her shamrock green eyes. She didn't bother to hide it from October either—he was the bane of her existence causing dark emotions to surge back to life in her head. "Thank you for once again ruining my life."

October fumbled with his thoughts, unable to counter her remarks. If he had left her alone, if she had ignored him then they wouldn't be doing the dance of avoidance. Or maybe, they would be doing exactly that. He wasn't even sure.

Five

When no one paid her any mind, Cat snuck downstairs in the middle of the night, made her special pie and went back to sleep. She was determined more than ever to avoid October like the plague—no matter how much pain it caused either of them. She got dressed after showering and brushing her teeth that morning. She wore a pale orange tank top, snugly hugging her upper torso with black leggings and her usual black cowboy boots. She made sure her leggings were the ones with the pockets for her wallet, key and phone.

She was groggy as her dark and thick brown curls were wild even after brushing them; fresh from the shower. She wore no makeup unlike Jade Devereaux who was into all that girly crap. She wondered when the youngest Devereaux sister would make an appearance as her brain stuttered over this and that. She checked the silver and black fridge making sure that her Orange Creme Pie was still where it belonged. She was relieved, thankful nobody had the midnight munchies as they were prone to do.

Cat poured herself a cup of hot, black coffee, drinking it while enjoying the burn of the caffeinated beverage. She was barely awake when the ginger ghost appeared in the doorway of the kitchen with this guilt present in his icy pale green eyes. "Speak now or forever hold your peace, Casper."

"I'm sorry, Catarina." October groggily spoke, half awake, half asleep as his eyes bore into the short, young woman. He did hope she could forgive him.

"Congratulations." Cat hissed, sipping some more coffee. She wasn't about to make the time to hear October out. She spent too much time reflecting on how bad things once were. She clammed up, shuddering at the memories that barely reached the surface. "Bro, just leave me alone."

"I'm not your brother, Catarina. Can't we talk about this like we used to?" October voiced, barely enough for her to comprehend him.

"I can't talk about what's past with you, freckle-faced demon. I have my own life to live. You ruined it once, you won't get that opportunity again." Cat informed October who dropped his gaze to the floor upon the cold, hard rejection.

"Catarina, please—" October opened his mouth to try again with the brunette who snorted in order to interrupt the ginger.

"Please, what?" Cat scoffed before a brief smirk lit up her face as she added an afterthought. "Please don't destroy…?"

Furrowing his eyebrows, October shook his head, becoming uncomfortable with her code words. "What is that? A band?"

"I have to go. I'm starting a new job." Cat easily lied to October who snorted. She was stopped by the ginger who grabbed the pie from her, holding it towards the ceiling. She bit the inside of her cheek. "Don't play with me!"

"I'm not playing with you, Catarina. You're playing against me. What were you saying?" October voiced, giving her a pointed look.

Cat sighed, jutting out her hip, placing a hand on her waistline. "I was just saying please don't destroy what we don't have. I thought of something funny and just dropped it to a short, incomprehensible question."

October lowered the pie, handing it back to her. "You're unbelievable, Catarina."

"I'm only unbelievable, because unlike you, ginger spawn, I'm not oppressed and uptight." Cat smirked, winking at October who winced at those words.

October's eyebrows pulled together. "Oppressed and uptight?"

Cat fully smirked with hurt flashing to life in her shamrock green eyes. As much as she shoved the pain down, she couldn't fend it off forever. She wondered if an elixir of life existed anywhere. "I'm sorry, October, but yes. You're oppressed and uptight—you always have been."

October pressed a hand to his head, pinching the bridge of his nose. When he removed his porcelain hand, she was gone along with his still beating heart. He slumped against the wall of the kitchen, allowing the frown to remain glued to his face.

Cat didn't bother to glance over her shoulder, aware that if she did; she would have to confront the pain sooner—no later. She could keep their memories together at bay for so long before the dam ripped itself apart. She waved to Tasmin. "I thought you left for work already."

"I thought I could give you a ride. Tavi is still sleeping off the crap Hunter put her through and October promised to keep an eye on her while we work." Tasmin replied as something crossed Cat's mind.

"Have you reached out to Jade about Tavi and her condition?" Cat inquired, causing Tasmin to snort.

"No, I haven't, Cat. Would you like to know why? Jade will turn up since we each received some type of magical curse...erm, gift." Tasmin briefly took a hold of Cat's shoulder before rushing to her purple convertible.

Cat joined Tasmin, cutting her eyes to the cobblestone house to see October standing on the porch. She saw fire burning in his icy pale green eyes as doubt, guilt, and pain clutched her heart once more. "I can't believe he won't get a life worth living."

"Your definition of a life worth living doesn't have to be somebody else's." Tasmin informed Cat, revving up the engine. She followed Cat's gaze to

October before paying attention to driving to work. "What happened between you two?"

Cat turned a scowl to the road ahead, toying with the idea of coming clean to Tasmin. "If I told you, Taz, you'd think I'm sicker than Jackie Chan fighting with his whole body."

"Sis, that's not true. Jackie Chan is a legend, especially in our household." Tasmin scoffed, playfully rolling her sea green eyes. She was in a purple v-neck tee shirt, black, fitting jeans with her brown boots. She wasn't feeling fashionable, especially not when it came to work.

"October and I have a history—a deeply personal, intimate, and heartbreaking history that goes back to our teenage years." Cat softly croaked as tears pricked the back of her eyelids.

Tasmin slammed her foot on the brake. She wasn't trying to judge her sister, but there was no way she heard Cat right. She groaned as her hair flew forward. "You were intimate with our step-cousin? He's related to us by marriage alone, but...what the actual—?"

The hot stray tears trailed down the tan olive cheeks of Cat Devereaux. They were the tears she had been fighting since the hurt October made her feel. "Exactly. I bought myself a one way ticket to the fiery depths of Hell."

Tasmin parked the convertible in front of the Clock. She clasped her hands together, eyeing the truck stop slash diner. She couldn't believe what she was hearing from Cat. Could she judge her sister for what she was telling her?

"You said it." Tasmin flung open the vehicle door, crashing it into a powder blue Mercedes that she had just pulled up next to. She began to grind her teeth while mentally cursing her family under her breath.

Cat hesitated to follow Tasmin, quick to exit the vehicle upon the Orange Creme becoming warm in her hand. She didn't have 'pie' added on the name like everyone else attempted to. Her creation was hers alone. She shot Tasmin a look. "Taz, don't hate me. He made me feel safe, secure, warm and hot in all the right ways. It was a long time ago and I'm paying for what we did."

Tasmin locked her convertible after writing a note to the person in the powder blue Mercedes, placing it under the windshield wiper. She proceeded to walk around, towards the entrance of the Clock, seething like no tomorrow. How could Cat drop a bomb on her like she had and expect her to be okay with it?

Cat delivered the pie, gaining a smile from the elderly woman who dished it out to the customers. "How many more will you need, Beth?"

Beth told Cat how many she would need. An Orange Creme each day before the elderly woman who owned the diner slash truck stop disappeared into the back.

Cat hadn't noticed how orange and white The Clock was until she stood present day in the joint. She cut her eyes around, scanning for familiar faces. She stopped short when she saw Theo sitting in a booth sipping on sugar flavored coffee with his opal eyes trained on a fiery, flaming Tasmin. Sensing that Tasmin wouldn't bother with her, she strode towards Theodore Wheeler. "Why are you making eyes at my sister?"

Theo had been smirking which soured before he gestured for Cat to join him. "I'm not making eyes at your sister. I'm waiting on a semi friend so we can begin discussing something that only we know about."

"I have nowhere else to be." Cat replied, watching the smirk return to the lips of Theo.

"Good, because you know my friend. I believe you met him either yesterday or the day before yesterday. It's hard to keep track of who you meet versus who you remember." Theo beamed, still sporting the red and black flannel checkered jacket that he had been wearing a day or two ago. It's how the man kept warm.

"Is this seat taken?" Gem Landry asked, appearing in casual clothes. His eyes briefly landed on the likes of Cat. "What's she doing here? I thought you and I were getting together in order to discuss the trials of the Harvest Sun."

"Cat doesn't bite." Theo replied, ushering for Gem to sit down.

Gem worked his jawline, no longer eager to befriend Cat. He had been looking into her background and her sisters. He requested to be the guardian of another, more reliable Faerie, but he hadn't been requested such a grant by the other Element Shifters. He was steelier than Cat had been towards October re-entering her life. "All in all, she shouldn't be here."

Theo scoffed, shaking his head at Gem. "You are aware that she probably should be present for this conversation."

"What is the Harvest Sun?" Cat is visibly irritated which increases with how Gem and Theo treat her. She poked the leg of Gem just to torment him. She hadn't been expecting an icy glare from the silver blue eyed boy. "I'm waiting."

"Theo, we can't work with a character such as Catarina Devereaux. Did you not read the file on her background that I left for you?" Gem muttered, thinking she wouldn't hear.

Cat cleared her throat. "If you would be so kind as to move out of my way, bussy, then I'd be leaving. Yeah?"

"Bussy." Theo repeated, making a mental connection. His opal eyes briefly shot Gem a warning look before he found his voice again. "Wherever did you hear that?"

"October from our teen days." Cat smirked, having looked up the word days after. He had always been a bad influence on her outlook of the world yet she let him in.

Gem's face darkened. "October Winston is the cousin she let defile her for how long...?"

"Step-cousin." Cat corrected, feeling the smirk fly from her lips upon Gem speaking her past into existence. "How do you know about my past?"

"He has to know about your past in order to work to protect your family. That's all I'll say about it." Theo voiced, not being one to judge as badly as Gem was.

"October is a blood relative of yours, Cat. He's a distant cousin on your mother's side." Gem muttered, extending a file towards Cat. He peeled it open, sharing the results causing Cat to almost stop breathing as the confirmation killed her.

Six

Cat was frozen, broken beyond repair. How could October Winston be her actual blood cousin? Gripping the edge of her seat, she vigorously shook her head—choosing denial as her best friend. Wincing, if she did digest it as the truth then she would be burning like no tomorrow. Is that why Tasmin had reacted to her news the way she had?

"Taz, what the fuck?" She approached the counter where Tasmin was serving customers. Her eyes held fresh tears stemming from disgust, betrayal and deep loathing for herself. "It's one thing to sleep with a step-cousin, but an actual cousin?! What the fuck?!"

"Quiet!" Tasmin hissed, throwing the washcloth down onto the sleek counter top she had begun to wipe down. She removed her white apron with an orange in the right hand corner. She gripped the shoulder of Cat, nudging her elsewhere so no one overhead, searching the devastated eyes of her sister. "I thought you knew."

Cat began to shake like a leaf from head to toe. "I had no idea which is why we crossed several lines as teenagers."

"You said you were intimate...you two, didn't...make love, did you?" Tasmin prodded, keeping a grip on her shaking sister. She saw the truth in the eyes of Cat who didn't hide the shame bubbling to life.

"We did and more than that—I even told him I loved him then." Cat hissed, unable to stop herself from shaking. She hated herself deeply from what Tasmin told her. "I'm an incestuous, disgusting, pig of a human being. I sold my soul to the devil."

Tasmin searched her brain for the bright side as she helped her sister sit down in a different booth. She rubbed soothing circles into the shoulder of Cat. "I bet you, mom, told you nothing about it. Look at the bright side, October is a very distant cousin."

Cat wanted to go home, curl in the shower and die. She couldn't stand herself, now that the actual truth is out there. Had October known they shared DNA? "Does he know?"

"I don't think October would have slept with you if he had known. He's not that weird and off putting." Tasmin whispered to Cat in hopes to calm her anxiety ridden sister.

Cat took deep breaths. It wasn't the end of the world for her. "I was in love with him!"

The whispered angered statement of Cat made Tasmin aware of something that her sister had long shoved down. She frowned after searching the eyes of her terrified sister. "And, you obviously still are in love with him—given your over the top reaction."

Cat's heart fluttered in a funny way that worsened the panic attack she was having. She was right when she said she ruined her life, but October had a major hand in fucking up her life. She dug her fingernails into her thighs, feeling the break of skin causing fresh tears to seep from her shamrock green eyes. "I am so fucking fucked—all the way to Hell."

"No, you're not, Cat. I know how you can save yourself and your reputation." Tasmin offered, having forgotten the warning brought to them by Sage Landry.

Cat wasn't entirely sure that Gem and Sage weren't one in the same person. She knew Gem said Sage was a clone built from his image, but how true was it? "What could possibly save me?"

"Date Simon. Ask for his forgiveness and take him out on a date. You could fall in love with him, have his children, and probably find a better job." Tasmin spoke, doing what she could to perk Cat up.

"I could also focus on the mystery at hand revolving around Sage Landry and the hologram of our Grandpa Morris." Cat pipes up, not wanting to think about romance. She had a good reason for ending her relationship with Simon and only part of it dealt with October. She wouldn't be able to give Simon Wheeler a life, but she could attempt to mend things between them.

"I would still converse with Simon. He could be the one." Tasmin rubbed the shoulder of Cat some more which did not help the erasure of October from her mind.

Cat could only get rid of October when she was distracted and he wasn't in her head. Otherwise, he lived rent free in her brain and she couldn't go there anymore—not that she should have in their teen years. "How about you? Who are you seeing?"

Tasmin scoffed, shaking her head at the absurd question. "The last guy I dated, which was three years ago, choked the life out of me. I almost died."

"I'm sorry, Taz." Cat croaked, seeing the darkness of a memory flash into the sea green eyes of her older sister. She hated being upset but she also hated causing the upset. "I'll talk to Simon, for sure and see if he can't forgive me for breaking his heart. He deserves better."

"That's it." Tasmin beamed, happy to forget about her personal life. She squeezed the shoulder of Cat about to get up when a particular person chose to clear their throat, interrupting their conversation.

"Ladies." Hunter Coleman cleared his throat a second time as he towered over them. He knew where they all worked. He wasn't finished with Tavi. "Where is my girlfriend?"

"She fled the state of Montana." Tasmin hissed as Cat watched him with cautious eyes.

Hunter was planning something. He drew up a tape recorder, setting it down on the smooth, marble of the flat surface. He eyed it then proceeded to eye the two oldest Devereaux sisters. "If what I'm hearing is correct, incest runs rampant in your family, ladies."

Cat's jaw dropped at the idea of some sleazeball like Hunter black mailing them. "What proof of incest do you have?"

Hunter pressed 'play' which reiterated Cat's intimacy with October who turned out by definition to share a distant blood connection with them. He pointed a finger at Tasmin. "I would think the two of you would know better than to play with each other. I can edit this to make it look a certain way."

Cat extended a hand, pressing a pointer finger to the tape recorder. She had no idea how, but she made sure the tape melted as a glow of light came from her finger. "You can't edit anything to make it look a certain way. What proof do you have, now, that it's melted?"

"Catarina Devereaux, I too possess magic—darker than yours; gifted to me by the devilish shadows. You failed my test, now, the world will see you as a mess." Hunter snapped his fingers, causing a spark of black between them. He managed to extract what was on the tapes to every radio station allowing them to hit 'play' which also made it to the television.

"That sounded like a spell." Tasmin quipped, beginning to grow panicked as the television was turned on for the customers to watch. Her sea green eyes widened when their conversation blared from the television, meeting their ears.

"Relax, Tasmin, it wasn't a spell. It was a curse. No man could want Catarina before, they won't want her after discovering her desire for her ginger haired cousin. Until you give me what I want, which is Tavi, then you ladies will suffer the consequences." Hunter said, beaming at the two oldest Devereaux sisters.

"I assumed the devil was a redhead. People like to portray him as blonde or dark haired, but gingers don't have souls. So, wouldn't the devil also be a redhead?" Cat asked in order to keep herself from falling apart in the wake of his havoc.

Hunter pointed to Cat, grinning. "The devil is actually a redhead. I knew I liked you, Catarina. It's a shame you have to see the dark side of me."

"You demonic son of a prick." Tasmin quipped, ignoring the exchange between Hunter and Cat.

"I am not a demon. I'm a shadow, completely different from a demon. The devil wiped out demons about a thousand years ago...well, his replacement." Hunter said, being as vague as he possibly could be. He enjoyed being vague while breaking the mold of Cat and Tasmin.

"We can't give you, Tavi. We won't—no matter what you throw at us. I'm still paying for the sins of yesterday, but Tavi, Jade and Taz won't pay to be abused, especially not by you." Cat comes to her senses, blasting Hunter with a ray of glowing light. She watched the man crumple into a pile of ashes before their very eyes.

Tasmin grew to uphold a stoic expression. "If October didn't know about the shared DNA, I'm sure he will, now."

"More conflict as if there isn't enough on our plates at the moment!" Cat hissed, sliding out from the booth once Tasmin had moved. She could hear the audio from the television which seemed to be on a loop. "It was a joke people! Ignore it!"

Tasmin shoved Cat towards the front door without realizing Theo and Gem had popped up from their booth.

Theo and Gem had been discussing the Harvest Sun, bearing witness to the magic of Cat which meant the other Devereaux sisters had magic too. They followed the two sisters causing Theo to catch sight of his powder blue Mercedes which was scratched and bent.

"Really?" Theo shrieked, causing Tasmin to freeze near the driver's side of her door. His opal eyes sought out the strawberry brunette. "Tasmin, you didn't—"

"No, she wouldn't. She let me drive in a reckless manner. I shoved her door into it upon arrival." Cat piped up, taking the blame causing Tasmin's shoulders to fall in a relaxed manner.

Theo shot Cat with an icy glare. "Cassandra is my livelihood!"

"Named after a Taylor Swift song?" Gem and Cat asked in unison causing amusement to surface in the silver blue eyes of the twenty one year old.

Cat had a challenge appear in her eyes.

"Damn straight, frodo!" Theo hissed, lightly slapping Gem upside the head.

"He's too tall to be a hobbit." Cat corrected Theo who didn't care too much about the references at the moment. She massaged the temples of her forehead as the reminder of their reality set in. "I will pay to have it fixed once I get my pay by the end of the week."

"It's bi-weekly pay nowadays which is why the economy has become shit." Tasmin informed Cat who snorted, horrified at the revelation.

"I can wait." Theo stated, sticking his hands into the pockets of his pants. He sighed. "We are coming with you—to your home. It's to ensure your safety. It's in our nature."

"We'll protect you and your sisters, but as for the sinner...well, she can fend for herself. Right?" Gem cut Cat with the sharpest glare he had given anyone.

Cat shot the blue eyed man, a bird. "I didn't know the truth at the time, so, if you hold that against me then you're trash."

"You still want him though, right?" Gem lightly teased as darkness surfaced on her face. His question was right as the heat rolled off of Cat in waves. He wasn't as dumb as Cat tried to play people it seemed. "I thought so."

"I can protect myself." Cat irritably groaned. "I can also help protect my sisters. Hunter Coleman has nothing to do with sins of the past or strained desire of the heart. He's a shadow."

"Cat, I'll protect you even if Gem won't. Nobody has any right to judge another—nobody's perfect. He's no better; he takes the cake on the sinning; real good." Theo spoke, being genuine. He didn't care what any of them did, protection from a shadow was vital, especially 'the lawyer' kind of shadow.

Seven

C at stood on the front porch once they returned to the house. She began to feverishly fidget with her fingers as her nerves ate the life from her. She couldn't face October with the truth present for the whole of Silver Hart to hear. She had further ruined her life and his by accident. She yearned to keep Tavi from the man who just about killed her.

The front door of the house opened, and out stepped the devil. His icy green eyes slid to her causing October to fold his arms to his chest. "So..."

Cat hesitated to cut her shamrock green eyes to the ginger who took up too much space in her thoughts. She squeezed her eyes shut tightly before releasing a lengthy breath. "So, did you know?"

"How would I have known that we actually shared DNA, Catarina?" October asked, sending chills down her spine. His voice was far from amused; deep and held a tint of annoyance. He was feeling exactly how she was feeling.

"I just...you're two years older than me." Cat spoke as if that explained why she assumed he would have known.

"My parents barely even look at me." October scoffed, sharp as could be, capturing her full attention.

He hadn't told anyone the truth about his parents. Why should he start?

Cat scanned October from head to toe as it hit her. "Don't tell me it's because—"

"My hair color embarrasses them. Neither my mother nor father have red hair." October voiced, scowling as Cat became anxious. He forced himself to look away from Cat, eyeing the green pastures that held a slight yellow tinge to them.

"How can they not have red hair? Are they even your biological parents?" Cat half squeaks as her face becomes a shade of pink. She was still watching him out of the corner of her vision while contemplating the real reason his parents could be embarrassed by him.

"They are. I did a DNA test a while ago." October muttered with furrowed, worrying eyebrows. He shook his head. "It didn't turn up anything about you and I sharing a blood connection. Are you sure it's even true?"

Cat couldn't be sure that what Gem, Theo, and Tasmin told her was even true. She only trusted her sister of the three, but even Tasmin could have been lied to. She wasn't that much of a sinner—she couldn't be. She sighed. "Where does the ginger hair come from then?"

"Grandma Silvia. She had the same shade of hair as me. Her eyes were a blue green mix, mostly blue." October mumbled, fond of his grandmother. He maintained a whimsical glint in his eyes while still staring out at the landscape.

Mindlessly, Cat extended a hand to his arm, lightly touching it before she shook off the idea of comfort. She didn't want to start something disturbing between them, especially with the truth clinging to the atmosphere. She caught his confused eyes, watching his lips spiral down. She dropped her hand from his arm. "I am so sorry. I—"

"You two may not want to be seen together." The voice of Gem Landry cut in from the doorway. He had quietly peeled open the front door, barely catching a lick of the conversation.

October looked at Cat before hesitating. He harshly gulped as the truth of his own emotions had sunk in long ago. He tore his gaze from her, numbly brushing past Gem. "Thanks for the reminder."

Cat's eyes followed October's every move causing another wave of hurt. How could she have fallen so far from grace? She met the silver blue eyes of Gem who was waiting for her to say something. "What?"

"Your sisters have shared some information with one another. To me, it's disturbing and gross. To you, it may be good news." Gem gently mumbled, shrugging his shoulders. He squeezed onto the porch as Cat headed for the entrance of the house.

Cat strode into the house, peeking into the living room. She found October had vanished, meaning he wasn't welcome into their circle of knowledge. "Taz? Tavi?"

Tasmin was sitting with Tavi and Theo. Her hand clutched their younger sister's hand who just revealed information to her that truly sparked concern. She motioned for Cat to come join them as Theo automatically stood up. "You need to hear this, Cat."

"I'm going to brew some herbal peppermint flavored tea. Do you ladies want any?" Theo hesitantly asked, seeming to freak out on the inside. He didn't get a response from them as he strode from the living room, down the hall towards the kitchen.

Cat furrowed her eyebrows at his odd behavior, shrugging it off. She walked over to Tasmin and Tavi, folding her arms to her bosom. She had been the one to become uncomfortable. "What's up?"

Tavi had joined Cat in her shame party. "I am a sinner."

"Wait..." Cat sat back on her knees. Instead of sitting down, she had crouched down while eyeing her sister. She hoped Tavi wasn't about to break her psyche. "Don't tell me you were intimate with our cousin too?"

"N-no." Tavi shakily responded, having heard the gossip over the television along with October. She had fumbled to shut it off, squinting her eyes upon hearing the news. Her sin was much different and way worse. "I...my sin isn't even close to yours, but it's way worse."

"Did you sleep with one of our sisters?" Cat raised an eyebrow, half joking as Tasmin swatted at her for the daft question.

"Can you not be disturbing for one whole second, Catarina?" Tasmin became irritable with Cat who smiled due to her unease.

"I'm pregnant." Tavi replied, breaking the discomfort in Cat.

"Who's the father?" Cat asked, not sure why she cared so much yet she did. Her sister could be in a world of trouble. She scoffed. "Is it Hunter Coleman? How far along are you? When did you find out?"

"Yes, Hunter is the father. Why wouldn't he be the father? I'm about six weeks and I found out when you two took me to Silver Hart Memorial." Tavi croaked, drained from relaying the message that she had already told Tasmin. She wasn't just exhausted from relaying such a message, but Hunter barely let her sleep.

"Boy or girl?" Cat asked, becoming flushed since she had her own fair share of secrets. She was going to be an Aunt—her sister announcing her pregnancy made it official. "I'm just irritably curious."

"I believe they said, triplets." Tavi uneasily voiced, sparking doubt in the heart of Cat. She released a shaky breath. "I'm hoping they misspoke. I don't think I could cope with raising triplets, especially by myself."

"Um, we're still here. You can stay with us as long as you need. Don't worry about the rent either; we'll manage to keep a roof over our head." Tasmin waved away whatever doubts Tavi was having.

October turned up with the tray of tea that Theo was attempting to help him make. He left the younger guy, pressing into the kitchen counter. "Taz, Tav, Catarina."

Cat rolled her shamrock green eyes at how he was still using her full name compared to Taz and Tavi. She shivered once his eyes bore into the back of her head. She sighed. "Tober."

"I don't like nicknames, Catarina. Your tea is piping so give it a few minutes to cool off." October spoke up, addressing Tavi who had silent, fresh tears streaming down her cheeks.

"Thanks, Oct. You're so sweet." Tavi croaked while Tasmin touched a hand to a chipped tea cup before extending one towards her.

Tasmin was impressed with the differing colors of cups. "Red, green and blue. Where's purple, O?"

"You'll have to shoot for the green. The blue is for Tav. And, we all know who the red belongs to..." October spoke up, saying what he said in the way he did to get under the skin of Cat.

Goosebumps infiltrated Cat as she shuddered at the wording. "What's that supposed to mean?"

"I think you know." October voiced before disappearing from their view. He didn't need Cat getting another word in edgewise.

Tavi sipped on the tea from the blue teacup which was a light shade of blue. She felt the healing properties of warmth light her up. She chuckled at the tension between the two whereas Tasmin ended up with a frown sliding onto her face. "You two should—"

"Tavi, no!" Tasmin hissed, pinching the arm of Tavi. She lifted her own teacup to her lips while Cat chose to forfeit her own.

Cat squished in between Tasmin and Octavia on the worn down sofa since crouching down began to hurt her lower to upper body. Hurt still remained in her eyes, because of the truth running rampant in the atmosphere. "You wanted me to talk to Simon, but how do you think that'll go over since what I've done is out in the open?"

"Catarina, if Simon is as sweet as we all know he is then I'm sure he'll understand." Tasmin tried to give Cat a pep talk, watching her sister frown.

"So, you're saying, a guy won't care if a gal hooked up with her cousin in their younger years?" Cat had to ask the question burning to life, searing into her mind.

"Given a good portion of guys usually do so without knowing just the same—I'm sure, Si, will come around." Tasmin voiced but even Cat and Tavi were doubtful.

"As long as you don't bring him home, Cat, you'll be fine." Tavi mumbled in a soft, hoarse voice.

Cat twisted a little bit to raise an eyebrow at Tavi. "Why can't I bring Simon home?"

"For the most part, October is living here now." Tasmin reminded Cat who knew that.

"I don't think you want Simon catching you watching every move October makes either." Tavi patted the arm of Cat who tensed in her spot at the mention.

"In what universe do I watch October? In any way, shape or form that's a weird notion. Have you seen him?" Cat scoffed, shoving down the truth for as long as possible. She admitted the truth once and messed everything up. Nothing good could come of reiterating the truth as a broke down twenty nine year old.

"I baked some scones." October popped in with a baking sheet of strawberry and blueberry flavored scones. He set them down on the coffee table, managing to graze the knee of Cat seeing her clench her jaw. He shot her an apologetic glance catching an overabundance of white rage present in her. "Is everything okay?"

Tasmin began to bounce her leg up and down. "Everything is fine. Why do you ask?"

"Catarina is overflowing with white hot rage." October nodded to the middle sister as Tavi slung an arm around Cat's shoulder.

"She's just coming to a tentilatingly realization. You know of Simon Wheeler, yeah?" Tavi spoke, yearning to be the one to clear up any confusion they still had.

Tugging at the collar of his white tee shirt, October lightly nodded. "Yeah."

"Cat is in love with him, always has been." Tavi spoke in place of her sister.

October became chilled to the bone. His blood boiled with anger that he was sure could be mistaken for jealousy. "Catarina?"

Cat didn't bother to meet his icy pale green eyes, sensing the betrayal she gifted him with. Her sister hadn't been lying though—she had been in love with Simon. She toyed with her fingers. "I'm sorry, but it's true."

"Look me in the eyes then." October croaked, half tempted to grip her wrists just so she would look him in the eye.

The sorrow Cat felt caused a few loose tears to slip free. She couldn't look him in the eyes, because the truth would further destroy them. "I have to go."

Eight

Cat was gripping a bouquet of light orange roses, nervously forcing a smile onto her lips. She tugged open the door of the Swift Rose, sucking in a sharp air of breath once she swung it off its hinges. She wasn't that strong, aware the hinges must have been a smidge too rusted. She was shaking like a leaf when she walked into the pub of her ex-boyfriend. "Simon?"

Simon had been wiping down the counter top, about to close up. His brown eyebrows furrowed as he heard her break the door. "Cat, what do you want? Why did you rip my door off its hinges?"

"It was an accident, Si." Cat softly mumbles, genuine when her eyes connect with his. She approaches the counter top to see him working his jawline. "I'm sorry."

"Was it an accident that you were intimate with your cousin?" Simon asked, glaring as sharply as possible at Cat. He searched her gaze for answers that long haunted him.

Cat set the bouquet of light orange roses down on the counter as her eyes dropped to her hands. "I d-didn't know that he was my blood cousin at the time."

"So, you would have still slept with him, right?" Simon didn't let up on his cold anger concerning Cat Devereaux. His heart thumped for her every single day of his life. What did he get in return?

"I..." Cat trailed off, meeting his gaze. Her eyes held pain beyond recognition. She hadn't meant to hurt him, but it wasn't solely October as to what made her break the heart of Simon. She had learned something when she was nearing the age of seventeen, a little before October Winston left her life—cold and even more empty than she felt.

"Incest is not wise—blood or otherwise. You're sick." Simon hissed, choosing not to give Cat a chance to defend herself.

"Si, I was young, dumb, and naive. I swear on the ginger spawn's life I didn't know. I couldn't love him." Cat spoke words—true and untrue, hurting herself further.

Simon bit the inside of his cheek. He lightly tapped his fingers on top of the counter. "It doesn't change the fact that you two..."

"Don't finish that sentence, Si." Cat's voice was strained as she decided to lay it on thick. "I was in love with you from day one."

Simon's breath caught his throat as he struggled to process her confession. "Why wait so long to tell me?"

"I...I learned something back then that has eaten me up from the inside since. I've told no one about it." Cat couldn't keep the sorrow from her eyes.

"What is it?" Simon asked, raising an eyebrow. He could see how pained Cat was, but would touching her give him a disease? He took a deep breath, extending a hand towards her over the counter, as close as he chose to get. "Tell me, so we can maybe heal as friends."

"I can't have kids—ever. I was told by a doctor when my mom took me to Silver Hart Memorial." Cat bitterly replied, taking a seat on a stool across from Simon who digested the news.

"What was the reason?" Simon asked, seeing more hurt flash into her eyes like she had no hope to carry on with her life.

Cat was beaten down, unamused since her life had been anything but grand. Her shoulders shook as she trembled with the memory of her brother beating her senseless surging to life in her mind. "My brother—"

"Let me get this straight, you and your sisters have an unspoken brother?" Simon shook his head lightly, allowing his brain to wrap around the new piece of information.

"He was the oldest of our siblings. Older than Taz who unleashed on him. She was sent to boarding school, because of her defense on my behalf." Cat shakily spoke as tears slipped from her eyes—not that she cared.

"He beat you until you couldn't carry?" Simon asked, taking a hold of her hand. He gave it a gentle squeeze, doing what he could to reassure Cat. He knew now how messed up she truly was with the reasoning behind it.

"Y-yes. He caught October and me cuddled together—nothing had happened, but numerous occasions produced a result especially without protection. He beat what was growing inside of me to a bloody pulp as well as..." Cat began to trail off, feeling even less human when the words left her lips.

"I understand. You don't have to finish. You can't have kids because he destroyed your way of conceiving while killing the unborn child of your cousin." Simon rattled off, clearing his throat as her pain twisted into shame. "God was trying to tell you something."

Becoming scorned with anger and cold, Cat quickly removed her hand from his. "I didn't come to explain to you for a lecture, Simon."

"You were hooking up with October while we were together, weren't you?" Simon quipped, changing the subject. He knew the lord almighty had everything to do with how messy Cat Devereaux was.

Cat bounced back, glowing in a light of gold. She couldn't believe she spoke to Simon as if he would dare understand her or what she had gone through.

Rolling her shamrock green eyes, she scowled at the man. "I would have thought you would be more caring, more compassionate."

"Cat, it's not my fault, you're the biggest whore or slut known to man. They both hold the same meaning, so much, like you and your non-tragedy, it doesn't hold up." Simon coldly remarked, leaving no room to be concerned for the woman. His livelihood had been stripped from him, aware that he should have listened to the rumors in high school.

"Si—" Cat opened her mouth to salvage what she had lost with him, but he wasn't having it. She closed her mouth once the man began to shake his head at her. She could tell the fight was over.

"Don't even bother, Cat. You may think you are Le Temptress, but you are far from it." Simon mumbled, shaking his head. He used a pointer finger to direct her from his pub. "Don't ever stop by here again. And take your pathetic ginger roses with you!"

Cat held a hand to shield herself from Simon who plucked up the bouquet only to throw them directly at her face. A blast of gold evaporated the darned roses causing her annoyance for Simon to further heighten. "I am not what you call me, just because you're spiteful."

"You are exactly that, Cat." Simon disagreed, feeling a flicker of relief once the sinner had left him to himself.

Cat managed to wind up back at the ranch house, skeptical about traipsing inside. She missed the sun sinking, kissing the world goodnight. She snuck into the house which was dead silent, shooting alarm throughout her body. She saw the faint glow of light emitting from the living room. "What's keeping you up this late?"

"It's only six thirty." October said, tapping the phone on the table, having just briefly checked the time. He was reading something, something important that dealt with their magic. His tongue peeked out with glasses glued to his face. He had yet to realize the disastrous way Cat felt.

"What are you reading?" Cat inquired, hesitating in the doorway of the living room. She had betrayed herself more ways than one in life, getting tired of caring about what everyone wanted her to be cautious about.

"The Grim was a hologram of your Grandpa Morris who ultimately opened up your world of magic, right?" October asked, flicking through golden pages scattered all over the sofa, floor and coffee table. Moving a piece of paper, searching for the one that stuck out to him is when Cat noticed the mess.

Cat ended up, inching closer to gather a better look at the disheveled living room—not believing her sisters aside from Tavi would allow October to be messy. "Why did you—?"

"Take a look at this!" October ushered Cat to join him, using a finger to motion her over while still not looking up.

Cat gave up in fighting a losing battle for a spare moment. She took the piece of paper, plopping down beside October who tensed when she pressed into him. She didn't care since she felt strained, drained, and ultimately done with it all. "What exactly is this?"

October gulped, noticing the close proximity as he leaned into her in order to eye the paper. He pointed to a written line without managing to touch her anymore. "Your Grandpa Morris isn't a hologram. According to these pages, his soul was trapped by the devil."

Warmth spread in the bosom of Cat who lifted an eyebrow, slowly lowering the paper to her lap. She chuckled at the absurd notion. "The Devil?"

October gently pressed a hand to her wrist, stirring emotions in them both. He wanted her to comprehend the fact that he was in no way joking. "Cat, I'm not joking."

Cat's eyes trailed up to meet the icy pale green eyes of October. She could tell they were both messing with their own heads via the closeness, feelings, and desire brewing once more between them. She shook her head, dropping her gaze from his. "Tober, the devil doesn't exist."

"Are you scared that if you admit that he exists, you'll burn for what we...?" Biting his bottom lip, October trailed off with his sentence, especially when his eyes landed on her body. He tore his eyes away, knowing neither of them should bother with their brewing torment.

A half smirk surfaced on Cat's lips. "Yeah, that's the problem. God already forced me to pay for our sins and with the conversation that was private playing all over Silver Hart—that mother is still making me pay. So, no, I'm not scared to burn for something stupid."

"What are you talking about?" October inquired, sensing there was something Cat hadn't told him.

Guilt, shame, anger, sadness swept into her eyes as she tore the piece of paper in her hand. Cat heard October gasp, but she didn't give a fuck. She was done with the games. "Tasmin only brought you here to invest in the ranch. Nobody really wants you here. You are absolutely meaningless to us—and stop being weird by looking into my family."

"Your family?" October heard the certainty in Cat's voice, confused by the sudden change in her behavior towards him. He finally realized that she had been hurting long before she joined him on the sofa. He saw the mess she was, grimacing. "I didn't mean to upset you, Catarina."

"You just pissed me off. Of course, I was already having a bad day. You should leave though—nobody has welcomed you here. Given the truth that surfaced, it's best for you to go either way." Cat spoke, smacking her lips with each word she spoke. She needed him gone to focus on her life and the weirdness that was happening with her sisters.

October extended a hand to her shoulder, feeling her tense under his touch. He sighed. "I can't leave like you want me to, Catarina. I already made a deal with Taz. You're stuck with me."

Cat heard the way the words fled his lips. She assumed he knew exactly what he still did to her, but she wouldn't allow it. She slapped his hand from her shoulder, standing up. "You should see a therapist about those issues."

October should have tore his eyes away from Cat, but chose to watch her walk away. If she was going to toy with him then he would match her game—stronger.

Nine

Theo was flipping through pages of protective circles, painfully aware that the Devereaux sisters needed protective circles in order to ward off Hunter Coleman. He was accompanied by Cat Devereaux who was currently breathing down his neck. He lightly ran a hand through his short, coffee brown curls before slamming the book shut. He shrugged. "This is a hopeless feat!"

"Why?" Cat asked, removing herself from her tippy toes. She had been avoiding October a week after the pain Simon reinstalled in her. She had been doing okay, coping while being sure to skirt around the likes of Silver Hart's favorite ginger.

"You won't stop breathing down my neck." Theo sheepishly mused, gaining an apologetic look from Cat.

Cat was in an orange crop top with an unbuttoned, open white cardigan. She was wearing light caramel brown, corduroy shorts with short, matching ankle boots. She saw Theo look her up and down. "What? Have you never seen a woman before?"

"I just hadn't noticed that you were one before today." Theo cracked a grin, teasing Cat who pulled her white cardigan closer together.

Cat shouldn't have to cover up for how discomforted she felt. She sighed. "Shouldn't you be looking at someone who fancies you in turn?"

"I do look at someone I fancy, just like you do." Theo spoke, shaking his head at the book. "There is nothing in this darned book about protective circles."

"You might not be able to put protective circles on us, Theo." Cat mused, nonchalantly shrugging her shoulders. She eyed the ranch. "This is some rather enormous land."

"I can't focus with you breathing down my neck, Cat. I could use a reprieve." Theo informed Cat, gesturing to her petite body. If he wanted to look at any of the Devereaux sisters—it was definitely Tasmin who did it for him.

Smirking to herself, Cat walked off, heading into the ranch house. She wasn't as cold as she should be living in Montana with the mountains. She poured herself another cup of coffee as she trekked into the kitchen, sipping on it from a pale mug, forgoing the red.

Tasmin was at the dining room table, staring at a handwritten note which kept her frowning. She barely paid Cat any mind who opted to circle back, sipping on plain, black coffee. "Cat, can you not drip all over the table?"

Cat hadn't seen Blu or Piper since the day of October's return, making her wonder if Sage hadn't caught up to the babies. She set her mug down onto the table, before joining Tasmin. "Tazzy, what's with the look?"

"October left this note for us, but it's not from him. It's from our least favorite person." Tasmin replied, tapping a finger on the note.

Cat threw a glance over her shoulder, not catching sight of the ginger she had been so careful to avoid. She was relieved, but confused since he had been hard to avoid in her teen years. She eyed the note. "What does it say?"

"Hunter Coleman wants us to meet him at Moonwick. It's the old camping ground that they are wanting to restore." Tasmin explains to Cat who sucks in a sharp air of breath before gently releasing it into the atmosphere.

"He wants us to bring, Tavi, doesn't he?" Cat asks, rubbing her face.

"He's not requesting her this time, but he wants you and me to meet him at Moonwick. We leave at midnight or else." Tasmin said, allowing Cat to read the handwritten note.

"We shouldn't go alone. Sure, we have powers, but we barely know how to use them." Cat hisses to Tasmin in a low whisper.

"Great idea. We should ask October to join us." Tasmin suggests causing Cat to scowl.

"We don't need him. We can call in Gem Landry—he's an Air Shifter." Cat offers a differing suggestion whereas Tasmin furrows her eyebrows.

"Cat, it's not up for debate. I've already discussed this with October. Gem won't work with us for two reasons; your fling with Oct and his guardianship simply extends to Jade. He told us while you were on the porch conversing with our cousin." Tasmin disregarded the fact that Cat grew clammy.

"I won't be able to go then." Cat said, needing to keep avoiding the ginger who invaded her thoughts and lived in her heart. She was certain he was going to cause her a heart attack.

"Cat, we have no choice." Tasmin mused, bursting the bubble of Cat. She eyed the clothes attached to her sister. "You may want to change or you may attract the wrong attention."

Tasmin was wearing a lilac dress that zipped up in the back, wrapped around her neck with an oval for her cleavage to be seen. Her dress flowed a little above the knees with a slit in the right side. Her shoes consisted of lilac ankle boots—a gift from Jade who was the fashionista in their family.

Cat became grumpy, gesturing to the dress snugly clinging to Tasmin. "Says the woman in a steamy dress that screeches take me."

Tasmin's face was coated with a blush. "I've been working with this guy, but I'm not sure he fancies me."

"Ned Tucker?" Cat snorts as the image of a toothpick thin nerd in black glasses surfaces. She knew the man was about five foot five with dark eyes, olive skin with a Greek history. She didn't see how he could be the type that caught the eye of her sister, but he was the only male co-worker at The Clock.

"He's adorable. His personality shines through—he gets really animated around computers." Tasmin dreamily voices. She gives Cat a thumbs up. "We are going on a date before the day is over."

"You and I could always go on a sister date instead so that we could discuss the actual type of guy you prefer; not some loser you pick up from work." Cat suggests, catching a reserved glance from Taz.

"I love you, Cat. I truly do, but not like that." Tasmin nervously voices as she continues to lay the lamest joke into Cat, feeling as if her sister deserved such a joke. "You are known for your blasphemous, incestuous ways. Sorry."

Cat scowled. "I just hooked up with my cousin. I'm not into incest."

Tasmin extends a hand to the shoulder of Cat, gently squeezing it. "I know. I was mostly messing with you."

Rolling her green eyes, Cat took a few deep breaths. "Should I join you at the Clock?"

"Didn't you already take in the Orange Creme?" Tasmin scooched back her chair, eyeing the time on her phone. She hadn't yet been to work which would give her time after to date Ned. "I gotta go. See you later and stay away from the Strawberry Cream—if you catch my drift."

"Strawberry Cream?" Cat called in question to Tasmin who was already rushing out the front door, slamming it shut. She sat at the dining room table, wondering what her sister had meant. She sipped more coffee as the day wore on. What could she do to pass the time?

She wiped sweat from her hands down her shorts upon standing up. She didn't need more anxiety inducing caffeine as she began to pace at the front of the Devereaux household. *What to do? What to do?* If she let herself sit around, her mind would go into spicy fantasies that she shouldn't have about a particular person. She was half tempted to leave the property when Tavi came bounding into view.

"Jade is coming home!" Tavi grinned, decked out in a sleeveless, strapless, all black, frilly dress. The top was heart shaped, cupping her breasts nicely allowing everyone to view them. It fell mid-thigh with black and white clad converse on her feet. Her hair was cleansed, revived with her feeling herself again.

Cat winced at the loudness of Tavi's shout. She scoffed. "What makes you say that?"

Tavi rushed over, handing Cat a note from their younger sister. "She's arriving sometime over the weekend—it's a permanent fix. I think some guy broke her heart."

"Who could have broken her heart? It's the other way around or have you forgotten?" Cat snorted, disbelieving that some guy could break Jade's heart. She knew how the younger Devereaux was—nobody pulled wool over Jade's eyes. "It doesn't say there's bad news."

"There's also good news." Tavi grinned as if her words made a difference. She saw the doubt plastered on Cat's face. "Cat, you know I'm hardly wrong about these things."

Choosing to be optimistic for the sake of Tavi and her babies, Cat smiled, slowly nodding her head in agreement. "Sure."

Tavi's face suddenly darkened as something crossed her mind. "Taz might disagree, but I'm joining you two at midnight to face off with Hunter."

"I don't mind if you join us, but you need to be careful." Cat mutters, wondering how Tasmin would take the news. She knew their sister would take it poorly since Tasmin was way too overprotective of her family.

Tavi chuckled, extending a hand in the air, letting loose a blast of darkness. She broke the vase their parents had loved all of their lives, beaming at doing so as if it was some sort of accomplishment. "I'm a grown woman. I can take care of myself."

Cat wasn't going to point out that before any of them had magic that they were all weak. She nonchalantly shrugged. "Prove as much to Taz and I'm sure she'll agree to allow you to tag along."

Tavi nodded. "I'll head over to the Clock as we speak."

"How about we don't head to the Clock as you speak? What if Hunter is lying in wait for you?" Cat raised an eyebrow, searching the gaze of Tavi who is giving her an expectant once over.

"You're joining me, Cat. I thought you knew this." Tavi explained, skipping over to the front door. She truly had too much prep in her step, flinging open the front door just as Cat burned her throat with the last remnants of her coffee, anxiety be damned.

Cat frowned, finding it odd how the coffee should have grown to be lukewarm since she had slowed down on drinking it. In fact, she began to pace, thinking she didn't need anymore so it had the time to cool down. She tore her eyes from the coffee when a shriek fled the lips of Tavi, abruptly stopping her hyperactive thoughts. "Tavi!"

Hunter Coleman had Tavi Devereaux pressed into his chest with an arm angrily pressing into her neck. He had shown up on the Devereaux doorstep to finish what he started. "You are coming with me."

Cat scurried into view, sliding to a stop, failing miserably as Hunter yanked her hand behind her back bringing her down to her knees. She couldn't believe her luck as anger and sadness swept her heart. "Let her go, Hunter! If you kill her, you'll kill the triplets she's carrying."

The grip Hunter had on Tavi loosened as shock filled his green eyes. "W-what? I'm going to be a father?"

Cat groaned, fighting against whatever hold he had over her. She shot a blast of pale gold at Hunter who side-stepped her sunlight with Tavi attached to him. "Let her go!"

Hunter remained in a dazed state of being. "You two are coming with me! You can restore Tavi's energy once she's tapped out, because where she's going—she's going to need it."

"Where are you taking her?" Cat hisses just as Hunter yanks her into him roughly, slamming Cat into Tavi. She groans from the pain as Hunter chuckles.

"You'll see." Hunter replied, disappearing in a fog of darkness taking the two women where he needed them.

Ten

"Bussy!" Cat shouted at the likes of Hunter Coleman who took her and Tavi to Moonwick. Her and her sister were placed under some spell to keep them bound to the grounds—long enough to get whatever Hunter was after. She was shouting at no one in particular since it was just her and Tavi; stuck in a set of pine woods with a hungry, dreary forest.

"He's a monster." Tavi whispered, half scared. Part of her wanted to reach out and break the nose of Hunter. The bigger part of her yearned to figure out what his plan was for her and her sisters.

"What guy isn't a monster?" Cat snorts, crawling over to Tavi since Hunter had instructed them to remain low on the ground and where he left them. She didn't mind if a wild animal ate her—at that point.

Tavi mirrored Cat in snorting once her sister crawled over to her. She did a double take, shooting Cat a weird look. "I'll tell you what guy isn't a monster. October and even Theo."

"Theo was at the house working on protective circles for us. He could have easily spoken to your ex-man about your whereabouts." Cat inheritedly disagreed with Tavi who shook her head.

"He also knew where we lived, because he had been living with me in the cottage house for years." Tavi said, being sure to cling to her sister.

"At least, one of my sisters doesn't believe all of what they hear." Cat rubbed soothing circles in the back of Tavi who didn't seem fond of the memories of being trapped in a house at the hand of Hunter.

Tavi bit her tongue on whatever Cat and October shared. She didn't believe speaking would help or hinder either or. She chewed her cheek feverishly, wanting the day to be over. "This is Moonwick? Looks drab for a campground."

Cat slowly nods her head in agreement. "As it should since it's older than the universe combined with star dust."

Hunter came back a few minutes before midnight to see both women where he left them. He rubbed his hands together, happy that he had them right where he wanted them. "I spoke to the devil and made a deal. He will spare me for the damage I've done if he can have Octavia Devereaux. He wants you."

"He can't have me. I'm an expecting mother." Tavi piped up, casting her navy green eyes to her stomach. She would think about her upcoming arrivals before she allowed somebody else to sell her down the river.

"Would you like some of my special tonic to help our babies?" Hunter questioned Tavi who grit her teeth at that. He had already gotten under her skin causing him to darkly chuckle. "You can't fight against your new destiny. Lucien Redmond will appear here in a minute to collect his betrothed."

Cat shook her head. "You cannot take our sister from us. Is this why you wanted Taz and I to meet you here—at midnight?"

"Catarina, you have no idea how lucky you, Taz and Jade are in all of this. He could have easily requested any of you." Hunter informed Cat, believing she would seem relieved. He noted how she wasn't relieved nor grateful for his intervention.

"Where is Tavi being taken?" Cat inquired, causing relaxation to seep into Hunter.

Hunter gestured towards the ground. "Tavi is going to the Underneath. You and your sisters can read about it once you find that dreaded spirit of your Grandpa."

"Are you trading Grandpa Morris for me?" Tavi quipped, aware of something Hunter had spoken into existence before their powers were returned to them. She recalled when they were stripped away, leaving them little to no room to breathe.

"Didn't I promise you that when the time came his spirit would be set free? Or do you want to risk him burning in the depths of the Underneath forever?" Hunter quipped, matching her gaze.

Tavi dropped her green eyes to the ground in order to process what they were hearing. She had agreed to accept her fate once the time arrived, but she didn't know how it would arrive. "What will you be doing in your free time?"

"I thought it was called Hell?" Cat did a double take, tilting her head up at the shadow.

"Nope. It's the Underneath and the flames that burn are a blinding blue—nor does it contrast or compare with that false Hades tale everybody keeps spreading. Lucien Redmond is the devil—his own kind of devil." Hunter went on to respond to Cat before she could put her spin on it. "I will be free to walk among your sisters, Tavi."

"Are you going to torment them?" Tavi asked with concern evident in her voice.

Cat scoffed. "He's got another thing coming, if he thinks he's going to torment us."

Hunter held up a finger, allowing a moment of hesitation. "I won't torment them as long as they don't torment me."

Tavi grew doubtful as a blue circle appeared around her. She hugged her legs to her chest. "What in the world?"

Hunter waved at Tavi as Cat released her sister, working her jawline at their soon to be parting ways. "It wasn't so nice to know you, Octavia."

Tavi was looking at her sister. "I love you, Cat. I know you didn't purposely sleep with your blood family. I hope we meet again."

Cat was alone with Hunter once the circle of blue around Tavi caught fire and saw the third middle Devereaux sister disappear in said flame. Her bottom lip quivered at how lonely things felt once she had no one to converse with. "Are you going to let me go?"

Hunter had his hands pressed down by his side as the second Devereaux sister got up. A smile broke his face as he paced in front of her. "I'm a predator. I need to have some fun with my prey first."

Cat could have told anyone that was in his sleeve of tricks. She shot a blast of gold light at the man, breaking that smile from his face. In her mind, she searched for an answer to the distaste of whatever a shadow was. She assumed light would be a weakness for the loser. "Eat daylight!"

Hunter winced, backing away, hissing as he got doused in her gold light. It wasn't enough to burn him, not sending him back to the Underneath. He ground his teeth. "You just initiated a war between us, Cat. I won't rest until you, Taz, and Jade are six feet under the dirt; withering away like Blu Devereaux."

Cat knew the name, but how did Hunter know the name of the oldest of her sisters? She nor Taz, Jade or Tavi found the time to speak about their past siblings that they lost. "How do you know about her?"

"One of many of my chronies did the dirty work. Ask anybody who knows me. Sage Landry sacrificed your horses for me—of course, he had been a clone of Gem Landry; serving for me until I didn't need him." Hunter irritably mused, upturning a palm to the skies.

Cat wasn't interested in knowing more or less about Gem let alone his clone. She sighed. "When did you stop needing them?"

"I stopped needing Sage once you returned." Hunter chuckled, becoming a smile of darkness before he vanished, barely leaving his Cheshire smile to creep her out.

Cat was once more alone again until the clearing of a throat startled her from her thoughts. She parted her lips, furrowing her eyebrows as she slowly reacted. She turned to eye October who frowned at the scorched marks of the ground. "Hunter—"

"I know, Catarina. I've been with you this entire time—just invisible, allowing you to ride off of my luck." October mumbled with his hands stuck in the pockets of his pants. He was in a pale green hoodie, chewing on his bottom lip.

Relief spread in Cat when realization slammed into her upon his closeness. She didn't have any more desire for him, as if it had evaporated upon stepping foot onto the campground of Moonwick. She could actually look at October and feel nothing aside from gratitude for him being a lesson. "Your luck?"

"I'm the Faerie of Luck." October once more murmured just as the crunching of twigs snapped nearby. His icy green eyes landed on Cat catching the relief in her eyes. He couldn't blame her, but he did nod to her cardigan. "Maybe, button up those bottom ones."

Cat didn't get a chance to respond when Tasmin came rushing into view with dirt staining her body and outfit. She forgot about the date her sister had with Ned. "Taz, what's with the new look attached to the outfit that Jade made you?"

"I..." Tasmin trailed off, casting her sea green eyes down at her dirt covered dress—thankfully she hadn't ripped it upon her fall into a bush with twigs moments ago. She had some leaves and twigs in her hair as if she was some crazy, woodland creature. "It didn't rip."

"Jade will be pleased. She was working on perfecting the material so you would have non-rippable clothes." October spoke up, half amused at Tasmin's concern.

"Where's Tavi?" Tasmin asked, cutting her sea green eyes from October to Cat.

"Hunter sold her to Lucien Redmond. The guy runs the Underneath so it's not Hell nor does it have orange flames." Cat informs the two who were late to the party.

"Correction, he promised Tavi to Lucien. He can't sell anything—he's a crooked lawyer and those punks lie all the time." October spoke over Cat, lightly nudging her shoulder. His correction of the younger brunette saw her roll her shamrock green eyes at him.

"Doesn't matter the wording, ginger saloon." Cat bit off, deciding to finish telling Tasmin what she knew. She clasped her hands together. "Lucien had our grandpa's spirit, meaning to exchange it for Tavi and Hunter will be tormenting us from here on out."

October managed to shoot Cat a sideways glance at a new quip she came up with on his behalf. "Was that meant to be an insult, Catarina?"

Cat went on to ignore October. "Our Grandpa should be roaming around these woods. I'm going to assume that if he's going to steal Tavi from these parts that he would return Grandpa Morris to the same location...or close by."

Tasmin gently nodded after processing the information they gave her. She noted the desire between the two seemed to have faded which was a relief for all parties involved. "How about we separate to find him?"

Cat said nothing as she went off in a differing direction managing to find herself amongst a set of bamboo. She shuddered as familiarity sank in as she walked a little further, coming to a stop in an opening. She twirled around in an oval shaped room with a worn down sofa in the middle. "Grandpa Morris?"

Grandpa Morris was a caramel-complected man with mint blue eyes. In his lifetime, he had been tall, but as it was—he was nothing more than a blue spirit; glowing a bit too much. "My favorite granddaughter!"

Cat flushed with embarrassment. Of course, she would rank as his favorite. She found it was vice versa on both of their parts. "Grandpa Morris, can we get you home?"

The man weakly stood up from the sofa, inching close to Cat. The man couldn't help shaking with wobbly knees as he slung an arm around her shoulder. "Be a dear and carry some of my weight?"

Cat began to sweat when Grandpa Morris put too much of his weight on her, but she pursed her lips into a thin line—not complaining.

Eleven

"Cat?" Tasmin asked a few days after they brought their Grandpa's spirit to the ranch house. She was cleaning up the busted lip of her sister who refrained from telling her how she got it.

Cat got into a fist fight with somebody she refused to talk about. She had been given a busted, bloody lip with a black eye on the right side. "I can't tell you her name. She wants me dead after everything she has learned."

"She doesn't know you. Only part of you." Tasmin said while Cat winced as she applied some healing solution to her sister.

"I'm sorry, Taz." Cat croaked, gaining a huff from her big sister.

"How about you make good on that apology by going and picking up Jade from Silver Hart University?" Tasmin raised an eyebrow, pulling back from her sore seeming sister. She extended her car keys to Cat.

Cat loved her family, but assumed Jade was grown enough to catch a ride or something. "I thought Jade was going to catch a ride. That's what I did."

"You two aren't one in the same." Tasmin spoke, shooting Cat a pointed look. She was tempted to tell her sister to have October join her, but didn't think it would be the best idea. She wouldn't want them to rekindle something sinister.

Cat didn't want company on the ride into town to gather her sister. She was at peace with doing things with no one around, having forgotten why she returned home. Having stepped foot onto Moonwick reminded her that independence was okay. "Hey, Taz?"

Tasmin quirked an eyebrow at Cat. "You're welcome."

"Thank you, but does the name Blu Devereaux ring a bell?" Cat asked as confusion worked its way into Tasmin.

Tasmin took a deep breath, placing the palms of her hands flat on the surface of the counter. "I...yes, Blu was our oldest sister. She was murdered in a gruesome manner then dumped at Moonwick. You were too young or too preoccupied to remember."

Cat pursed her lips, choosing not to hold the confession against Tasmin. How could she? If it was at the time Cat thought it was then she had definitely been preoccupied. She wiped her hands down the vibrant red tank top, covered by the black denim jacket she wore. Her Jean shorts of denim were also black, leaving room for some imagination. "I'll go retrieve Jade."

October had just appeared in the doorway of the kitchen. His hair was messy with sunken eyes. He looked like a disaster with his flannel jacket hanging half off his left shoulder. "Hey, ladies..."

Tasmin quirked an eyebrow. "October, what's wrong?"

"I was replaying a ton of bad memories in my head on repeat. The more I tried to shut them out, the louder they became." October muttered, barely awake. He didn't even really notice Cat who was gawking at him like he had lost his everloving mind. He could care less about anything at the moment.

Cat sighed once his breath wafted over to the two women. "Your breath smells of alcohol."

"Cat." October's eyes half widened as he cast them towards her. He was certain she was a figment of his imagination so early. "When did you get here?"

Cat opened her mouth to make a snarky comment, but shoved it off. She frowned, shooting Tasmin a brief glance. "Make another pot of coffee. It seems Jade is going to have to be late for her homecoming."

"October is capable of—" Tasmin was about to protest, but saw the glint of annoyance in Cat's shamrock green eyes.

"Do you not remember the time at scout camp when he was fifteen? His circle of daft friends convinced him to try alcohol for the first time—it was his first and last time. He was left to stumble through the day with no help." Cat irritably explained, angered at the foul memory. She had stepped in that night to help him overcome it, because it didn't seem the effects desired to wane off by themselves.

"Sure, Cat. Help October, but when you're late and Jade yells—she ain't yelling at me. Are we clear?" Tasmin said, jutting out her hip.

Cat extended a hand towards October, nudging the ginger to turn about face. She walked with him, making sure he didn't stumble into the living room towards the fireplace so they wouldn't catch fire. Managing to get him up to the bathroom wasn't even the biggest chore about his hunger over disaster. "Tober, you have to shower and brush your teeth!"

October snorted. "How about I just sit on the floor and wait for a better life to kick in?"

"If you don't get your unlucky butt up, I will kick you." Cat groaned, hating the fact that once she got him in the bathroom, October sunk to the floor like the mess he was presenting himself as.

"You'll kiss me?" October asked, tilting his head sideways at her in a funny manner.

Cat placed her hands on her waistline. "Don't be weird. We're past that stage."

"Nothing good can come of me getting ready for another terrible day." October groaned, shutting his eyes. He brought his knees up to his chest, burying his face in his pants.

Cat was beyond disappointed in October. She had been present when he vowed not to ever touch liquor again. She wasn't about to tolerate his self-sabotage or his messiness. "If you don't get up, I'll let you ruin what you can fix. I don't want to have to look after somebody who is capable of looking after themselves."

"I'm not asking for you to look after me, Cat. Just leave!" October hissed into his knees. His voice was strained, barely audible as Cat rolled her shamrock green eyes to the roof of the bathroom.

Cat crouched down, gripping the shoulder of October. She squeezed it in the hopes of getting October to quit being so down on himself. "Tober, look at me!"

October resisted the urge to look at Cat. What would be the point of meeting her eyes? He didn't feel like being hypnotized by her beauty even further, especially given the circumstances and truth. He scoffed. "I'm good."

Biting the imaginary bullet in her head, Cat hesitated to press a hand to the side of his head. She barely smiled when October tensed at her touch restoring the hurt of losing half a soul between them. She sighed. "October!"

Wincing at the shout of a strain she placed on his name, October removed his face from his knees. His pale cheeks held tears streaking them as he forced himself to look her in the eye. "I cannot—"

Cat gave him a pointed look, cutting him off by pressing a finger to his lips. "You either will or you won't join me to pick up Jade. I'll probably need backup so either pick yourself up or you'll have more to deal with then the pain of loss. Are we good?"

October felt a surge of a pulse course through his veins once more. He stood to his feet, slowly nodding. He was assuming she used her powers given to her on him. "O-okay. Fresh air would do me some good, probably even help slay the memories."

Cat dropped her shamrock green eyes to the marble, sleek, beige floor of the bathroom. She points to the shower. "You hop in the shower. I'll go grab you a fresh pair of clothes."

October saw Cat toy with an idea that she kept unspoken as she shook her head with a scowl forming on her dark pink lips. He missed her. He let shame flood him at the very thought as he focused on what they were meant to do for the day. "Yes, ma'am."

Cat waited for October to turn on the water, mixing it in sync before she made a beeline for the bathroom door. She heard the discarding of clothes once she was out causing a panic attack to take hold of her. Why did she agree to let him join her on her road trip? She didn't want his company nor could she keep it. She wandered down the hall, entering his bedroom—on a mission while focusing to get to her sister. She didn't know how they were going to get Tavi back with no sign of Hunter as of the moment.

She plucked up an outfit with boxers and a different jacket for October—doing so in a mindless manner. She chose to wait outside of the bathroom door for when he got done. She wasn't about to step into the bathroom with any kind of male showering, shuddering at the disdain it brought her. She was stroking the set of clothes as Tasmin called that the second pot of coffee was ready when they were. She wasn't about to leave the house with October's breath smelling like alcohol though just as the water of the shower came to a stop.

October opened the door, plucking the clothes quickly from her arms before closing it once more. He dried off, got dressed then proceeded to frown. He leaned on the counter of the black and white sink, also, made of marble. "Um, Cat...?"

Cat rolled her eyes, hearing the hesitation present in his voice. She snorts. "Are you dressed and appropriate?"

"Why wouldn't I be?" October called in turn as the doorknob twisted, turned and revealed the brunette. His throat bobbed with a gulp once she entered.

Cat lifted an eyebrow. "Have you brushed your teeth?"

"Not yet, but I—" October replied, shaking his head as he picked up a red and white toothbrush. His icy green eyes were on his attire in which Cat ignored his issues in her mindless choices.

Cat walked over, plucked the toothbrush from his hand, found the toothpaste and stood on her toes while pulling October closer. She began to brush his teeth, interrupting whatever he found wrong with his clothes. "I don't care about your appearance. I have to get my very much late arse over to Silver Hart University—you are wasting my time, but that's what you're good at, right?"

October shuddered, taking a hold of her wrist with the toothbrush. He shot her a look before spitting out the toothpaste proceeding to gargle with mouthwash. Afterwards, he cleaned off the toothbrush, set it back where he plucked it from and kept his glare on her. "I don't waste time, just because I'm human."

Cat processed as much while his hand still gripped her wrist the entire time. She shrugged as her eyes slid to his outfit of a red and black flannel jacket over a white tee shirt with dark pants. She made a face as she eyed her own outfit. "I wasn't even looking when I picked that out for you. Sorry."

"Can you stop being so uptight? Last night was bad enough." October gently mused, watching her eyes soften at the reminder of how bad his head had been. He sighed.

"Wait..." Cat struggled to free herself from her grip as irritation and realization sparked to life in her brain. "Wait...the red and white toothbrush brush is mine. Yours is green and blue. What the fuck?"

"I'm a mess." October noted, patting the top of Cat's head before brushing past her. He didn't care, but she did—so he paid her back for her smart remarks and angered quips. He wound up in front of Tasmin who held a black thermos towards him.

"Jade texted and she's not happy." Tasmin informed him just as a dazed and confused Cat joined them.

Cat watched October guzzle down some of the coffee, snorting as it scorched his throat. She smirked at the return of nature doing its work. "Are you done trying to choke your throat with burns? We have somewhere to be."

"You can't drive, Cat." October felt even more relief wash over him once the coffee hit his system. He made sure to remind her of the fact while needing to add another blow to her morning. "You hitched rides to the ranch, or did you forget?"

Twelve

Clean air, blue buildings and excitement stemmed from driving into the heart of Silver Hart. A couple or two held hands as they walked on sidewalks past thrift stores, book shops and whatnot while confusing the likes of Cat.

"I thought you had to drive all over Silver Hart." Cat stated, matter of factly.

October chose to drive in place of Cat, sure that he wouldn't crash. He took his black car, casting Cat a glance once he parallel parked. "No, Silver Hart is pretty walkable. The university is about a block or two up ahead, down the right."

Cat smiled over at October. "Good one."

Unbuckling his seatbelt, October flung open his car door once shutting off the engine. He briefly cut her one more glance. "You just had to match us."

"You just had to use my toothbrush!" Cat hissed, forgetting the seatbelt had her strapped into the car after flinging open her own door. She slammed into the seat causing her breastbone to come alive with pain.

"Cat, are you okay?" October hurried around the car to make sure she was okay. He saw her clench her teeth; her breathing was a bit shallow, stirring true regret for his disastrous morning. He leaned in the passenger side, hovering over Cat as he clicked the button to release her. "I am so sorry."

"Please don't." Cat muttered in between shallow breaths. Her heart had picked up speed from the slam, but her being distracted by October was her own fault. She had one task that she was failing to accomplish. She was trying to let the pain subside before making any quickened moves. "I'll wait here for a second and catch up to you. You go meet Jade or she will have our heads on a platter."

"I can text her. I'm not going to leave you, Cat." October informed her, reaching over her once more. Brushing against her, still had some effect on her as it did him. He wasn't stupid or blind. He held the thermos towards her. "Maybe, this will help."

"I appreciate the gesture, October, but caffeine is loaded in that coffee. I don't need my heart racing further into death." Cat barely spoke as October got busy texting Jade who fired off a very hostile response. She scoffed as October hovered over her so she saw the exact, menacing words of her baby sister.

Cat started to feel a smidge better, groaning as October fully stood to his height outside of the car while she climbed from it. She shut the door. "You probably should have mentioned you were alone since she had that response."

"As I told Jade, I haven't touched you since you told me you loved me then ran." October didn't look over his shoulder at Cat while typing another fast reply to the hostile Jade Devereaux. He snorted. "You were sixteen. I was—"

Cat let him interrupt himself while feverishly texting Jade like it would matter. Shaking her head, she began to take great strides down the sidewalk; reaching the end while October hung back. She glanced to the right, parting her lips once she discovered that the ginger had been right. "Oct...are you kidding me?!"

October hadn't noticed her choice to retrieve Jade. He gave up typing, stuffing his phone in his jacket pocket, finally looking up to see Cat waving from the corner at the end of the street. "So sorry."

Cat was annoyed with her arms folded to her bosom while glaring at him. "Instead of pissing her off further, allowing her to think what she wants to think...how about we actually show up to retrieve her?"

"Good idea." October quickly nodded, leading the way to the silver bricked campus making Cat's eyes water. "Brighter than my hair."

"Agreed." Cat coughed, wishing the building was a darker shade of red or black. She saw the fuming Jade Devereaux as she appeared next to October. Her sister's nostrils were flaring with widened, fiery mint blue eyes.

"She's definitely going to kill us." October whispered down to Cat once his eyes landed on the five foot one, twenty one year old.

Jade Devereaux was slim and slender—the most beautiful of all her sisters. She had a head full of lengthy, black waves with full, dark pink lips and olive skin. She was in a silky white skirt with an emerald silky tank top. Her shoes were white ankle boots, making a diamond look rough in comparison. She had luggage by her side with a white and ruby encrusted ring on her left finger.

Her eyes came across October and Cat on the other side of the road, stopped by the oncoming traffic. With her nostrils flaring, her menacing gaze set on the devil of all time—October Winston.

"October, you're too sweet to include me, but her fiery glare is set on you. Whatever you did, just apologize." Cat lightly nudged October before crossing the road without a care in the world. She was closely followed by the ginger just as Jade's temper flared higher.

"I love you, Cat, but if you can't be on time to pick a sister up from college, you won't be on time for my wedding either." Jade said, snorting as she briefly hugged Cat. She then eyed October from head to toe. "Why are you matching with my sister? Have you not done enough damage with your twisted lust?"

"It took two to tango. We were young." October spoke with a coldness in his tone towards the younger Devereaux. He didn't hate her, but it was clear Jade hadn't ever liked him. He got tired of trying to please any of them.

Cat kept quiet on the past, doing a double take with Jade. "Your wedding?"

"You two aren't just picking me up. You're also picking up Bellamy Clark—my future husband. We're engaged to be married this coming month." Jade said with an accent so southern; her tone confused Cat.

Cat chuckled. "Um——?"

"We're only staying at the ranch for the wedding then we're moving down south to Georgia." Jade squealed with delight. She was beaming like there was no tomorrow. She tapped her watch. "Bell will meet us at the Moonlight Café for a late dinner then we can go home."

Cat became stoic, searching her mind for the likes of Bellamy Clark. Her eyes narrowed at something Jade once told her when Jade was just nineteen. "Whoa, what the actual fuck?"

Jade winced while October flinched at the loud question fleeing the lips of Cat. "Yes, I'm marrying a professor."

"You've known him for two years! How do you know you love him?" Cat hissed, slapping Jade's arm.

Jade fired back the glare of daggers, more icy, less friendly. "He's twenty seven and I met him on my first day of college when I was eighteen."

"Oh, so, you've known him for three years and he's a predator?" Cat snorts, feeling her eyebrows meet her hairline.

Jade yawns. "At least, I'm marrying somebody who isn't family."

Cat had the strong desire to rip off the ear of her younger sister. "I'm not marrying anybody in the family—blood or not, you sick, bitch."

October could feel the thickness of the atmosphere thanks to a testimony yearning to suffocate him to no end. He shook his head, lightly scratching his short, messy curls. "Okay, tempers are high, but you're family. Cat, you should be happy for Jade. Some people know when they know."

The chill Cat sent October's way should have been enough to keep him from digging more of his own grave. She did a double take before forcing a false smile onto her face. "You know, what, Jade? You two can ride back together. If you two are staying under the same roof where I should be then I'm done."

"Cat, you know what it's like to be in love. Some people can make things work when they're both willing." October spoke, ignoring the last bit that she spit at them. He wished she would calm down and quit being so over-dramatic.

"Do you want me to prove you wrong?" Cat growled, not wanting to be nasty with either of them. Something was happening that made impulse thrive in her veins. She was beginning to believe it was the fresh air of being at the heart of her hometown. "I need you to leave me alone for the rest of my life. I'm done with the cult we're in."

"Cat!" October hissed in warning to the brunette, but she was already walking off from the way they had come to get Jade. He watched as she made it to the end of the corner, but she kept walking instead of taking the turn back to his car. He slapped a hand to his forehead for how she could be at times.

"Cat will be fine. She always is." Jade said, swaying October from going after Cat. She beamed up at October who was confused by the notion.

Cat walked and walked until she caught sight of an apartment complex across from a rather gorgeous library. She found herself breathing in the lightness of it, putting her at ease. She had been off and short tempered while dealing with October in the morning anyway, but why? She was on the cusp of plopping down on a bench under a tree when the apartment complex further drew her in. She tilted her head at the odd name; **Air Loft**.

A woman of about five foot four with a slim, but curvy figure appeared in front of Cat when she walked into the lobby of the apartment complex. The woman had sun-kissed skin with hazel blue eyes and her short, dirty blonde hair framing her cheeks perfectly. She was in blue and white with makeup coating her face. "Can I help you?"

"I am so sorry. I just wandered in. Something about the name just drew me in." Cat sheepishly apologized about to leave when the woman at the desk chuckled before the blonde shook her head.

"No, honey, that's not how it works. When you are drawn into this particular apartment complex, you don't leave feeling as you did before." The woman spoke, maintaining an audible English accent that you had to listen closely for her. She sort of sounded like a walking, yet slightly aggressive teddy bear.

"Sure." Cat agreed out loud as her heart thumped with a nerve wracking sensation. She had been called to the complex, so, what would be the harm in checking it out? She cast her eyes for the name of the blonde, not finding a name tag or plaque. "What's your name?"

"Oh, just, Colette." The woman shook her hand before proceeding to also sign to Cat, allowing another realization to fling itself into the mind of the brunette. She raised an eyebrow. "Who might you be?"

"Oh, it's just Cat." Cat spoke, sticking her hands into the pockets of her black denim shorts. She felt like a change of scenery would be welcome. If she could escape the ranch and stay away then she might be safe to have the life she always craved. "Do you have anything available?"

"I do have one spot open. It's near my apartment. Follow me." Colette signed, motioning for Cat to follow her.

Cat didn't think anything could go wrong, not caring if it did. She followed Colette to an apartment that drove her to buy it outright. The money she produced was just enough, stemming from the past few weeks of her Orange Creme selling. She sighed. "I think I'll need to find a new job."

"You're welcome to work for us as a desk assistant. I own Air Loft—for several reasons." Colette suggested, gaining some relief from Cat.

Cat wasn't quite sure what she wanted to do where work was concerned. She didn't want to work, baking pie made of oranges and its juice forever. Her singing dreams were long over and she had become quite okay with that. "I might have to take you up on that offer."

Thirteen

Relief clutched her heart when she was gifted a silver key to a one bedroom, one bathroom, cheaply rented apartment. She was in **5B** which had powder blue walls with silver powdery blue carpet in the living room. Her eyes narrowed at the spacious open kitchen with dark oak cabinets with sleek, white counters. Sure, it was small, but to her it was as cozy as could be. She noted a small fireplace with a mantle which sort of reminded her of the ranch house.

Cat was certain she would be okay, able to start over without guilt touching her. She had been eyeing the space of the living room, decorating it in her mind's eye. She didn't hear the door creak open or the gasp that fell from the lips of October who had been able to easily pick out where she vanished. "It's so breathtakingly beautiful."

"Dangerously so." October agreed, finally breaking Cat from her dreams of future happiness which did not include the ginger in it. He barely caught the questioning gaze she sent him. "The lady at the desk wouldn't shut up signing about it—she seems deaf-ish."

Unable to contain her excitement, Cat smiled, meeting his gaze. "It's mine. I'll be moving in here so I won't have to deal with you, Jade or her whatever. I'm done with the unhappiness everyone has bestowed upon me at the Devereaux Ranch. D-O-N-E."

October heard Cat loud and clear causing his icy pale green eyes to search hers. "So, I've made you unhappy? I apologized for this morning. How many times do you want me to say it?"

"I don't want you to keep repeating the same boring mess, October. I want and need change. I crave it. I deserve it." Cat was sharp as a tack with October who released a small, depleting breath.

"Do what you think is best, Catarina, but I definitely won't come for you." October informed Cat in a nonchalant, indifferent tone.

Cat felt a slight sting, shrugging as she let the separation fully commence between them. "That is part of the whole point of me vacating the premises of my own home. Or have you not been paying attention at all?"

October took a minute to register her words. He didn't believe it and wouldn't. He wasn't the reason she was moving out. He shared moments of wellness with her. "Lie to yourself if that's what saves you."

"Actually, we all know who saves me and it's not myself or lies." Cat grins, wiggling her dark brown eyebrows at October.

October was baffled for a second until he realized what she was on about. He rolled his icy pale green eyes at her. "Clark Kent isn't real nor is the actor who portrayed him in Smallville. You're insane."

"Maybe." Cat was still grinning, feeling at home as her eyes scanned her newly bought apartment once more. She saw the disapproval in his eyes. "You aren't my type. You were a mere distraction of boredom. How much more transparent do I have to be with you?"

Quirking a barely visible eyebrow, October knew better. He turned around to exit the apartment, muttering incoherent whispers to himself as he went along.

Cat continued to smile with relief remaining within for a minute or so before she stepped out, shutting the door in order to lock **5B.** Her mood hadn't soured until the person on her right stepped out of his apartment. She frowned, scurrying after October only to bump into his backside.

October groaned, sharply twisting about face. His eyes scowled down at Cat before flitting up to meet the guy coming their way. "Dude, you seem familiar."

"I'm an Air Shifter and the guardian for Jade. I should seem familiar." The unamused voice of Gem Landry rang out, startling Cat into a new world of quiet. He shook hands with October who extended a hand to the brunette over Cat's head.

Cat winced, wanting to be gone. She needed to pack what little she returned to the Devereaux Ranch house with.

"I'm October Winston. I'm the cousin of the Devereaux clan." October replied, gaining a scathing look from Gem who cut his eyes to Cat.

"Gem Landry." Gem spoke, wiping his hands down the front of his shirt with disgust smeared all over his face. "You two may want to seek therapy or counseling for your disgusting ways."

Cat flinched as if Gem had spit on her. She saw the confusion slither into October's eyes before he grew cold towards the blue eyed male. "It's not...we aren't—"

"You were. You even confirmed it with Taz. Don't you recall what was all over television and radio two weeks ago?" Gem said, seething as he cut his eyes from one to the other. He gestured between them. "Here you are...what, hooking up in my face?"

Cat whirled on Gem, slamming a blast of light into him. She startled the brown haired male who gasped as pain erupted in his chest from the impact. She wasn't having anymore jokes from a past fling come anybody else, especially when she was dissecting the problem. "I'll have you know that we were young, nothing has happened since or will ever again. If you or anyone keeps making the same joke—they'll feel my wrath as their last breath."

The full, pink lips of Gem became dry, chapped, and even cracked from her gold light. He could barely breathe while being unable to answer her. He slowly nodded while a frown escaped October.

"I think you're on the verge of drying him to death, Catarina!" October hissed, attempting to pull her from pressing Gem into the wall by her apartment. In doing so, Cat whipped around and punched him with her fist engulfed in gold light.

Cat was the cause of the ginger stumbling, falling and gushing blood right before her eyes. The pain she thought she had slain resurfaced when his icy pale green eyes seared with hatred from her action. Her tongue became tied, heavy as she rushed from the building, needing to escape.

"Cat!" Gem called after her once the dryness seeped away. He saw the hate in the eyes of October, but it was worse—it was hurt, loss and the longing of non-existence. He truly felt bad for the ginger whom he tried to help from off the ground.

Colette watched in amazement and astonishment as Cat went whirring by. She got up from the desk, scrambling after the brunette who stopped by the grass, becoming sick. She frowned, tutting at the upset woman. "If you get sick on it, you pay for it."

Tears were streaming down the olive face of Cat as she puked until nothing was left in her stomach. Her tears were silent, but hot as she rolled to sit on her butt instead of pressing her knees into the grass that she fell too. Her eyes met the blonde who blocked her sunlight. "I'll clean it up."

"No, you won't. The janitor will. He gets paid for what he does and how he does it." Colette informs

Cat, taking a seat next to the brunette. She wondered what had upset the younger woman. "Penny for your thoughts?"

Cat was having a day, mostly bad, but she was to blame. No one else could be blamed for any of what had happened aside from her. She was evil, they were all starting to make her see the truth. She wiped away loose tears as best as she could. "It's got flaming hair."

"This is about a guy?" Colette snorted, cutting her hazel blue eyes to Air Loft just as October peeled open the lobby door; made of ectoplasm glass. She inhaled sharply.

"It's about a guy and a sister." Cat half mumbled, following the sound of the slamming door. Her eyes should have stayed on the ground beneath her.

October had this unattainable anger that had him fuming all the way back to his car. He caught sight of Cat from the corner of his eye with Colette before he kept walking. If she was going to be violent and mean then he didn't care what became of her. He slid into the driver's side of his car, half tempted to let Jade find her own way back to the ranch house. In fact, he almost convinced himself to pack up and leave Silver Hart.

Cat couldn't slay the shame as hard as she tried. Hurting somebody verbally was different than outright hitting them. Even if she could, she didn't want to look October in the eye. What good would it do either of them?

"I'm sure your boyfriend will be fine." Colette yawned, having watched the fuming ginger only for him to scurry down the sidewalk.

"He's not my boyfriend. He's my cousin." Cat scowled as fresh tears pricked the back of her eyes.

"Oh?" Colette signed with her brows intermingling. She didn't see any resemblance between them, believing they were a couple. Even she could tell that the eyes of Cat were a differing green. She shook her head. "Really? You two don't look alike. Are you sure you weren't raised with lying parents?"

"It wouldn't matter. He would be my step-cousin by marriage even if we didn't share a blood connection." Cat felt torn on the subject as the tears flowed freely without her knowledge.

"Why don't you take a DNA test? It would solve whatever conflict you two have—part of it. Relationships by marriage shouldn't matter especially if you're an adult with no actual blood ties." Colette suggested, doing what the blonde could in order to cheer up Cat.

Cat sighed, inhaling sharply to take a deep breath. She slowly exhales, slightly feeling better. She was ready to lay in the grass for the rest of the day as a chill sent shivers down her spine. "You're right. It might help, but after I punched him..."

"Give it time then." Colette suggested, slinging an arm around Cat's shoulder in order to rub comforting circles in her skin.

A loud horn blared behind them belonging to a particular black vehicle.

"Catarina! Get your ass up!" October growled in the direction of the two, grown, childish acting women on the grass. Him honking had startled Cat enough to cause her to jump—the yelling just escalated it.

Cat let her eyes flit to October who was spewing for an argument or fight. She took note of his posture causing her to become less fierce and more anxious. "Colette will—"

"Nope, dear, Catarina, we have to meet Jade and Bellamy at The Moonlight Café. It doesn't matter what you want, it's not up for discussion. Hop in." October stoically replied, nodding towards the passenger side of his car.

Cat shakily brushed herself off, shooting Colette an apologetic glance. She saw an idea take root in the hazel blue eyes of her acquaintance. "I'll see you around?"

"Sooner, maybe." Colette said, wiggling her blonde eyebrows at Cat.

Cat nervously approached the car, about to slide into the back when October cleared his throat.

"Catarina, you're up front with me. No ifs, ands or buts about it." October was strict while his voice came out in an icy tone towards Cat.

"I could easily walk to The Moonlight Café." Cat's response to October was clipped as could be in turn to the ginger.

"Do you want me to exit this vehicle, pick your ass up and force you into the passenger side?" October asked, not looking at her. What would be the point of looking at her? He would just get more tense, stressed, and angered by her appearance.

Without another word, Cat wandered over to the passenger side, feeling about as unwelcome as a cat entering a bird cage to eat it. She placed her hands down in her lap, staring directly at them the entire drive to the Moonlight Café.

Fourteen

October had become unhinged. His icy green eyes held a glint of crazy in them like he was about to ruin everything. He was starting to really terrify Cat who shouldn't have punched him. He clung to her wrist when she tried to get up to go to the bathroom. "You can wait until our arrivals appear."

Cat sat back down beside October. She didn't utter a word nor did she glance in his direction. She was scared of what she would find. Her eyes scanned the silver and purple cafe with a full moon, hanging on the wall. "Who could have come up with such a hole in the wall place?"

October ignored Cat. If he spoke it wouldn't be the answer she sought. His leg began to bounce up and down, grazing her leg.

"There you two are!" Jade beamed upon bursting into The Moonlight Café. She spotted them through the window—pressed into the long running silver booth. Her happiness about stopped at seeing the craziness present in October and the discomfort in her sister. "Are you two fighting?!"

"No." October replied just as Cat disagreed with a "yes."

Jade face palmed. "I know you two have your issues, but I don't care. You two cannot be fighting or arguing right now. Do you hear me?"

Closing the menu, he had been leafing through, October's icy green eyes slid to Jade as he lay the menu on the rectangular silver surface of said table. "I told you, we aren't fighting."

Cat rolled her eyes. "If we weren't fighting then he wouldn't act like he could control me going to the bathroom."

Jade glanced at the wrist October had belonging to Cat. She snapped her fingers at the ginger. "Quit being a possessive, immoral idiot and let her go to the bathroom."

Cat felt October's reluctant grip loosen on her wrist as shame once more flooded her better senses. It was the shame she felt for punching him so viciously. "Thank you."

October scowled after Cat, not saying anything else as Jade coughed to gather his attention. He turned it to her, furrowing his eyebrows.

Cat slipped into the bathroom, taking a few deep breaths in order to breathe. She leaned on a porcelain sink allowing her eyes to trail up to the watery, silver mirror in front of her. She quirked an eyebrow upon watching a ripple effect take place before her via the mirror. "Unbelievable." She proceeded to use the bathroom then wash her hands and dry them. She could have sworn she heard a faint, elegant string of giggles rolling out of the mirror.

Shaking her head, she had to get back to the others, becoming confused once she sat back down near her irritated captor. Her younger sister grinned, clasping her hands in unison.

"As I was telling dear October, Cat, Bellamy is sweet, handsome, one of a kind." Jade gushes, opting to act like she had some kind of bragging rights. Her eyes were glossed over, having jumped to the roof of The Moonlight Café.

"Where is this Bellamy Clark?" Cat asked, sort of suspicious of her sister. She nearly shrunk where she sat when her eyes met the steely green of October. It meant that he had the same question she did on behalf of somebody they had yet to meet.

Jade checked the time. She held up a finger before pulling out a watery blue flip phone, opening it to dial Bellamy. "Hey, Hon! Where are you? We're waiting on you!"

Cat leaned in closer to the table just to be sure she could hear the deep, gruff voice belonging to Bellamy roll out of the other side. She had become suspicious of Jade which couldn't have been a good thing. She gripped the leg of October in the process who was still very much unenthused with her. "He does exist then."

"Why would you think I was making it up?" Jade quipped, being snotty to her sister. She flashed a grin at October who proceeded to grimace.

October couldn't answer Jade due to their brief discussion once Cat walked off earlier. He wouldn't as she sat back causing him to clear his throat. "Could you please remove your hand from my thigh? It's unbecoming of a woman."

Wincing from his tone, Cat shakily removed her hand from his thigh feeling even guiltier. Rolling her shamrock green eyes she saw a familiar woman stumble into The Moonlight Café with a wicked grin splashed on her face.

Colette had red lipstick with purple eyeshadow to accentuate her features as she stepped into the joint. She was in a snug, tight fitting deep blue dress that fell a little above her knees. Her shoes were a matching set of blue ankle boots with a purse clinging to her left shoulder. She had an idea on how to kill the brewing feud between Cat and October. "Hi, lovelies!"

Cat felt relief flood her heart. If her new acquaintance joined them then she wouldn't be alone with the red viper and the snake next to him. "Would you care to join us for dinner?"

"Yes." Colette quipped, aware of how fantastic she appeared. She scurried over, nodding to October. "I need a seat next to big red."

Jade vacated the spot she had taken beside her cousin. She sat across from October while Colette plopped down next to him. "You got a thing for redheads?"

Colette snorted. "No offense, Red, but I prefer them tall, dark and handsome—as most women tend to."

"You wanted me not to be offended?" October inquired, gaining a nod from Colette. The craziness in him had worn off, having been brought to life by the punch from Cat and the anger it twisted in him. He hadn't felt so angry in his life except for a few rare occasions.

Patting his shoulder, Colette sent the ginger a crooked smile. She gestured to his hair. "Could I get a lock of your hair, Red? It's for an experiment from this theory I have. I haven't met a real redhead up until this point."

October groaned, shrugging. "Fine, but—"

Colette leaned towards his hair, lightly snagging a piece of it with ease causing him no pain. It was a part of her air magic causing her to shoot the confused redhead a weak smile. "I have air magic."

"Air Magic allows you to snap hair from somebody's head without harm?" October snorted in disbelief.

Cat had been soaking in the conversation while her eyes cut to Jade who was fuming beyond repair. She wondered what the conflict was with her younger sister. She hadn't known Jade to be a brat, but she was sure acting like it. "Jade?"

Jade shot Cat a nasty glance. "What do you want, Cat? You should know better than to steal everyone's spotlight."

Cat frowned, yearning to head to the ranch house to collect her things. She didn't feel safe under the heated, rage baited gaze of Jade Devereaux. She nodded. "Keep thinking that. I don't want your thunder or anyone else's thunder."

"My powers are easy to use. What can I say?" Colette asked, waving to the waiter for a shot of raspberry flavored alcohol. She needed to forget the anger seeping from the pores of Jade. "You three do realize that this place is intended for those with magical gifts."

"I knew that." Jade smiled, happy to have some knowledge that Cat didn't.

Cat just shrugged. She cast her shamrock green eyes to those in The Moonlight Café, catching sight of Gem Landry at the bar speaking animatedly to someone. She didn't see any signs of Theo with Gem. "Elements are magical?"

"Always have been. Think about nature and how things happen without the aid of humanity." Colette beams, taking the shot and downing it.

Cat understood her implication as her eyes remained on Gem. She should have noticed his casual clothing options earlier; when she first encountered him—he looked like he worked on a farm. "People can be snakes."

Jade scoffed. "Only an attention seeker would voice that crap out loud."

October began to bounce his leg in annoyance just as a man with short, black curls entered The Moonlight Café with honey brown eyes hidden behind gold spectacles. He pointed to the well dressed man with a half smile once his eyes set on Jade. "Is that your man?"

Jade followed October's eyes to the entrance causing her eyes to widen with enthusiasm. She feverishly waved to Bellamy. "Bell!"

Bellamy had been scanning the place for his fiancé with his eyes lighting up once she called his name. He threw open his arms once Jade bounced from her spot to throw herself into him. "I have missed you, sweetheart!"

"Obviously not when she was hitting on me earlier." October irritably muttered under his breath. His whisper didn't go unheard by Cat who snorted.

"Excuse you?" Cat managed to slam her leg into October's who frowned. She watched as October slowly, but surely looked her way once more.

"Excuse me for what, Catarina? You're starting to get on my nerves." October began to seethe as his icy pale green eyes locked with hers. He knew she wasn't about to shrink this time as her own anger flared.

Before Cat could form any type of sentence, Bellamy and Jade approached the table—sliding across from them. Narrowing her shamrock green eyes at Jade, she grew deeply disappointed in her younger sister. "So, this is the predator you're marrying?"

Jade gasped, disgusted by her older sister. "Can you not be sick at the table, Cat? You have secrets too."

"My secrets came out along with my dignity all over Silver Hart or did you forget that?" Cat wasn't playing with her sister anymore. She didn't know why Jade had a problem with her, but the younger Devereaux did. "You're very disgusting, Bellamy Clark. Using your power to lord over someone's head."

Bellamy frowned, trying to take the insults in all good fun. He folded his arms on top of the table, directing his gaze towards her. He had broad shoulders, standing at about five foot ten. He was handsome, no doubt about it. "I'm sorry that you have experienced trauma, Catarina Devereaux and you are taking it out on others, but that is not an excuse."

"Bell isn't wrong. You cannot tell somebody how to love, Cat." Jade snorted, briefly cutting her eyes to October who had his eyes on the table before him. A pout stirred on her lips. "You can't tell somebody who to love, not with your track of incest."

Colette cleared her throat at the precise moment only to snort. She took another shot, standing up for Cat; not even knowing the younger woman. "Track of incest? As far as anyone knows, it's only wrong if there's proof that there's a blood connection. Do you have proof? Family by marriage doesn't count, especially if there is no blood between them!"

"Tasmin confirmed it, didn't she?" Jade felt scorn due to Colette sassing her in front of the guys at the table. She didn't care that she was being sassed by Colette in front of her sister.

"She confirmed it with proof of blood?" Colette quipped, shutting Jade up. She scoffed, nodding. "I thought so. None of you have any proof, but are willing to judge what you think you heard."

Pride blossomed in the bosom of Cat who was grateful for the ironic blonde. She could tell they were going to be friends, just by Colette's stand up for her alone. She didn't have or want friends up until that point. "I'm glad somebody cares to be on my side. Thank you, Co."

Fifteen

Cat fumbled to exit the black car of October once he drove them to the Devereaux Ranch. She lightly shut the door with no more anger in her heart, as of the moment. She wound up leaning on the hood of the car just as Jade, Bellamy and October removed themselves from it. She could feel the piercing eyes of October as something in her had changed. She had been in love with the ginger, but she had changed over the years.

Her love for the one who clutched her heart had been on its deathbed, still dying. Her arms pressed into her chest as October cleared his throat. She didn't quite meet his gaze as he leaned next to her. She felt the warmth they always shared spark to life, starting a new fuse. She saw Jade and Bellamy kissing their way up to the front door of the ranch house.

"I'm sorry about punching you, October. If I could go back to the before of my action, I'd punch myself. You were the one person I didn't ever want to lay my hands on in such a devious manner." Cat hoarsely spoke with a crack of pain in her apology. Her eyes glistened as tears threatened to spill from her eyes once more.

October had been holding a grudge on Cat's behalf over the punch. He was allowing it to slip away, especially when he spent more time with Cat. He knew she hadn't meant it, trying to break a solid bond before it could lose its life by itself. He brushed a hand over her shoulder. "Cat, would you look at me?"

"What's the point?" Cat asked, holding back the tears threatening to spill over. She craved the notion of curling up on her bed in a ball so she could sob herself into the ground. She was fairly certain she didn't want to live anymore, not solely, because of October either. She always felt so strongly; depression could be a blessing for her, but it was the greatest curse she had experienced all throughout life.

"Cat." October softly mused, gathering her teary eyed attention. He proceeded to pull Cat into him for a lengthy, much needed embrace. He massaged soothing circles in Cat who couldn't help but sob into his white tee shirt underneath the black and red flannel jacket. "It's okay, Cat. I promise."

Cat wasn't one for tears. She hardly cried so sobbing into October's arms made her dislike herself more, but after it was all said and done; relief embraced her heart. She sighed, drying her eyes once she pulled out of his embrace. "I'm sorry."

"I'm sorry too, for my hand in our past, holding a brief grudge over the punch and the fact that I can't stop loving you. It will get better." October mumbled, watching Cat recoil further from him. He raised an eyebrow. "What did I say?"

"You know what you said." Cat sadly voiced, shaking her head as she walked around October. She walked right up to the front door of her house, twisting the doorknob to enter. She sure was going to miss her home that October and Jade were so keen on driving her away from.

October internally slapped himself once he realized his slip up. He made sure his car doors were locked before following Cat. He caught her before she could be seen by Tasmin or the others. "I didn't mean for that to slip out, Cat. I'm sorry for everything including my slip up."

Cat took a shaky breath at the entrance of the door. She only nodded to acknowledge his words, not wanting to agree or disagree with him. She knew how she felt about him, like she was ready to take the leap and move on as she should have done when she and Simon started dating. Instead, she had been wrapped in red the entire duration of her relationship with Simon.

"There you two are!" Tasmin hissed, appearing at the entrance of the doorway. She saw the sadness seeping from the pair causing her to shake her head.

"You can entertain Jade. I'm just here to pack up my things." Cat informed Tasmin who became alarmed.

Tasmin shook her head before her eyes burned into October. "What did you do?"

"It's not what he did. It's what I did and how I can't breathe in this house any longer. I'm an adult, I need my own place, my own space to breathe and create. This isn't it." Cat huffed, just as October hesitated before lightly brushing past her on his way to the living room. She once more watched him walk away, further hurting her.

Tasmin sighed, following the shamrock green eyes of Cat to October. She didn't want to be left to live alone with October, but it would beat living at home with no one else. She slowly nods, taking one of Cat's hands in her own. "I'm so sorry, Cat. Couldn't you have talked this over with me first before making such a decision?"

"What about Tavi who's still stuck in the Underneath with the Devil?" Cat quipped, gently gnawing on her bottom lip.

Tasmin frowned. "There's not much we can do about getting Tavi back with little to no information."

Cat barely patted Tasmin's hand before dropping it. She nodded while giving her older sister a pointed look. "I'm going to pack what little I own. Jade has become a nasty cretin since she began college. I don't recognize the sweet, young woman who wants to have her way with our cousin, just the same."

Tasmin quirked an eyebrow. "Really?"

Cat went to pack her stuff just as Tasmin rushed to view Jade attempting to tease October who was tense with unease. It didn't take her long, aware that she would need a new toothbrush. She made sure to pack a sleeping bag since she couldn't move furniture plus she craved being out of the house as soon as possible. She reappeared in the doorway of the living room, frowning upon Jade trying to press into October while her fiancé just smiled as if encouraging it. "Jade, your man is on the sofa, not clinging to the fireplace trying to escape your crude gestures."

"Weren't you leaving?" Jade rolled her mint blue eyes at Cat. She would do what she wanted, how she wanted as concern had laced the icy green eyes of the ginger.

"I'm still leaving, but hands off the ginger." Cat quipped, briefly glancing at October. She found it one thing to accidentally sleep with your possible blood and another thing to do so on purpose. She wasn't sure what was up with Jade who once upon a time wouldn't have done such a thing; blood or otherwise.

"Come, now, Cat. It's just a bit of fun." Bellamy said, gesturing for Cat to chill.

Cat met the eyes of October who looked ready to flee the scene at any minute. He looked as if he was begging for help when he gave her a look. An invisible smirk attached itself to her lips. "Are you enjoying yourself, ginger rose?"

October opened his mouth to speak when Jade snorted, shaking her head at her sister.

"Of course, he's enjoying himself. He's a bigger freak than you are, Cat, evidently. He'll probably take anything he can get." Jade spoke in place of October.

October frowned, shaking his head in disagreement. "I beg to differ. You're engaged to be married."

"I don't mind. The more, the merrier." Bellamy said, patting his lap just as horror flicked to life in Tasmin.

"No." Cat informed the engaged couple. She jabbed a finger in the direction of October. "He's my ride to my new home. I no more can drive then—"

Jade yawned so loud, she made sure to interrupt Cat. She shrugged. "Your bad driving is no one else's problem."

Cat rolled her shamrock green eyes. "Are you ready, Tober? It'll be dark soon and I definitely don't want to be stuck with the newly cemented devil."

"You would know if I was the devil." Jade beamed, wiggling her eyebrows at October. She had to add something else to make everybody's skin crawl. "The devil has the same colored ginger mop of hair as your lover."

Cat wasn't about to listen to anymore of her sister or her crap. She clasped her hands on the cusp of burning Jade alive. "I didn't threaten you earlier, but would you like me to chip away the last bit of light you barely have?"

October parted his lips, setting his drink down on the mantle. He had been handed a glass of champagne by Jade once he walked into the living room, having been holding it while sloshing the liquid around. He hadn't even drank it, recalling the earlier moments of Cat threatening Gem then punching him. "We should be on our way, Cat."

Cat was about to smirk when October reached her, ushering her from the living room doorway. She saw him make the connection from earlier, a moment she semi forgot about it. She slid back into the passenger side of his black car. "If you didn't want to be put in such a position, you could have easily walked away."

"Did you ever think that maybe I wanted to be in that position?" October replied in turn as he slid behind the wheel of the driver's side. He barely cut his eyes to the brunette as something occurred to him. "Jade was a close second for me, always has been."

Cat worked her jawline. She was about to slap him due to his words. "That young? And, I thought, Bellamy was the predator."

"I'm not a predator, Cat, but she is quite the stunning beauty. You all are." October said, stirring more unease within Cat.

Cat couldn't breathe as the words he spoke took root in her brain, returning the hurt she felt moments earlier. She couldn't believe she had listened to his fake apology. "Can you just drop me at Air Loft and be on your cherry way? I cannot stand you anymore than I have forced myself to. I was in love with you, you never loved me. Thank you for the reminder."

October scoffed. "I didn't say—"

"Just drive." Cat croaked, yearning to be parted from October forevermore. She wasn't about to partake in his shenanigans for the rest of her life. Every time she thought they were making progress from the past, he chose to burn it to the ground like the soulless creature he was proving to be.

"Catarina, could you just take a minute—?" October was on the brink of asking Cat a question when she slammed his car door so hard he felt it shake. He became irritated once all four windows shattered from her anger of the slam. He had no sooner pulled up to the Air Loft than she was ditching him for something better which wasn't nothing new for her.

Cat flipped October the bird as she stormed into the lobby of Air Loft which is how one got to their apartment. She saw Colette behind the desk, still in her stunning dress as she eyed the sign in sheets. "I'm moving in with the bare minimum."

"Sure. If there's anything you need then let me know. Those DNA results should be in to me in about a few days—tops." Colette signed, causing Cat to nonchalantly shrug.

"I don't care if they come in clear, proving that he's not my blood cousin. I don't ever want to see October Winston let alone think about him ever again." Cat mumbled, heading to **5B** so she could start her new life.

Sixteen

Colette was smiling about two weeks after Cat had moved into her apartment. She hadn't seen any sign of the twenty nine year old so she went to check on the brunette. She was standing in the doorway with a tool belt, hard beige hat and a plunger for the toilet. She saw the disheveled brunette who looked unusually pale like she wasn't healthy. She had been yearning to tell Cat the good news concerning the DNA results over October.

"Cat...erm, what's with the ghostly appearance?" Colette eyed the woman who clung to the bed sheets wrapped around her body. She noticed the gaunt eyes with white skin and a cold sweat. "Are you trying out for the role of Casper?"

Cat yawned, shaking her head. "No, I've just opted to let myself slip away. Nothing good happens when I try to live or be happy."

"Come off it!" Colette hissed to Cat as she ventured further into the apartment of Cat. She saw no furniture with a sleeping bag sprawled out on the living room floor in front of the fireplace. She shook her head at the vacancy. "This place could use some sprucing up. A touch of home, should do."

Cat nonchalantly shrugged. "I just want to go back to bed."

Snapping her fingers, Colette was able to conjure a well furnished apartment for Cat. She did so for all their tenants since it was in the contract. She beamed at a flabbergasted Cat once a powder blue sofa appeared in front of the fireplace. "I do it for all of my tenants."

"Thank you, Colette." Cat gently mused, just as another knock came from the front door. She watched the blonde peel open the door to reveal Gem on the other side.

Gem had his hands shoved down into the depths of the dark blue jacket he wore. He was biting the inside of his cheek. "Could you two keep it down? I'm trying to rest for the busy night ahead."

"Meet at Midnight?" Colette inquired, gaining a reluctant nod from Gem. She knew that Cat wouldn't comprehend a lick of what they were talking about.

"Yep. I'm trying to get answers. I don't know who sent the shadow, but it definitely wasn't...*him*." Gem informed Colette, being careful with his words. He finally took note of the horrible state that Cat appeared to be in. "What's wrong with Cat?"

"Nothing that won't be solved by tonight. Can we join you? It would probably help Cat heal from everything and move on." Colette muttered while Gem shrugged.

"If you think it will help. I don't think a club overflowing with magic will help, especially **Meet at Midnight** where everybody is drawn to every body."

Gem half hisses to Colette in a low whisper. He was an exception to the rules of the magical club, feeling nothing for anybody.

"Gem, she could use it. Look at the state she's in!" Colette hissed, gesturing to Cat from head to toe.

Cat had been shivering, managing to drop the bed sheets to reveal her messy, loose state further to Gem by mistake. She saw the grimace twist his lips before he nodded.

"Bring her." Gem said, shutting the door as he went so he could go chill in his apartment.

Cat was aware of one shadow. Her sister had been ruined by Hunter who sold Tavi to the devil. If she could uncover who the devil was or how to get where he thrived then maybe, she could save Tavi from her newly cemented fate. "I'm going to shower and change."

"I'll make us a cuppa." Colette grinned, wiggling her eyebrows at Cat as something surfaced in her mind. She had to call after Cat who went to the bedroom where the bathroom connected.

Cat was so zoned out that she didn't hear a lick of what Colette said. She rummaged through her clothes, picking up a green, white, and red checked dress that would fall mid-thigh, hug her body and had thin straps with a zipper in the back. She eyed a note attached left to her from October. "Come what may." She crumbled up the piece of paper with three words, tossing it in the trash as she headed to the bathroom with a pair black strappy high heels.

Once she showered, and dried off, she got cozy in the dress with heels. Her eyes landed on the mirror as she fished for red lip gloss with a hint of blush and light lavender eyeshadow. She was tired of everyone's voice in her head telling her that she wasn't good enough. She rummaged through her bag once more, picking up a black denim jacket—another past Christmas gift from her former lover. She was glad she wouldn't be running into him anytime soon or she may have to kill herself.

"Did you hear me?" Colette asked, sliding a cuppa towards Cat who plopped into a stool across from her. She was sipping her own with a cube of sugar, milk and honey.

Cat just added a cube of two sugars, wrinkling her nose in disgust. "No peppermint? I fancy the peppermint flavored tea—hot, above all flavored tea."

Colette shrugged. "I'm happy with the original."

Cat slid her arms into the black denim jacket as she toyed with the small spoon in the mug of tea. "Did I hear you about what? I was zoned out the entire time."

Colette grinned, removing a piece of paper from her pants pocket. She would have to return home to get ready for heading to the club. "I was hoping you heard me. This might help you overcome your conflict with October. You two do not share any blood—whoever was told confirmed a notion without proof let alone the facts."

Cat eyed the paper that Colette slid toward her with the truth written on it. She gently squeezed her eyes shut, soon folding the paper only to shrug. What could she do with the truth, now, that it was a fact that they weren't related by blood? She didn't think it wise to go back even if she wanted. "Oh."

"I emailed the radio stations and television that played that horrid message with you and your older sister; I'm assuming, about you sleeping with your cousin; confirming that you did not sleep with anyone in blood connection and family by marriage only counts when you're young—not an adult." Colette eagerly informed Cat, further making her want to die.

"So, everyone will know that I'm not incestuous then? That's the only good part." Cat mumbled as Colette's grin spread.

"I sent a copy to everybody all over Silver Hart including October so it'll clear up your confusion." Colette voiced, seeing anger, hurt, and betrayal surface in the shamrock green eyes of Cat.

Cat had fresh tears escape her, but they weren't tears of relief. "I don't care. I know you were trying to help, but I can't just jump back into things with October—blood or not. He told me I wasn't good enough the last time I saw him with him wanting Jade instead. They all want younger; never their age."

Colette frowned at the mention. "I wish I would have known. I would have torn up the results, Cat. I'm sorry."

Cat could tell that Colette was genuine. She wiped away her tears before they could ruin her natural, light makeup. "Are you going to attend this magical club dressed in shorts and a white tank top?"

Colette finished her cuppa, holding up a finger to Cat as she rushed towards the front door. "I'm on your right when you first exit, but when you first enter on your right is Gem. It shouldn't take me long."

Gem was leaning on the wall across from Cat's apartment, waiting on the two women while lost in thought just as Colette peeled it open. He jumped in place from the start of the blonde, briefly catching the hardly enthusiastic Cat on the stool at the table of her kitchen. "Is she okay or is she still in a bitter, dull mood?"

Colette cleared her throat, leaving the apartment door to Cat's place open. She called to the brunette to ask if Gem could come in. "Gem wants to come sit with you. Would you be alright with that, Cat?"

Cat barely threw a glance over her shoulder at them while nonchalantly shrugging. She didn't know if she cared what anyone did anymore. "That's his call."

Gem pushed himself from leaning on the wall, walking into the apartment of Cat. His deep blue eyes were burning into her backside, wondering how she could be so clueless in her personal life. Then again, what did he know about personal or love? He was so shut off, and cold towards the world that he didn't slow down to allow emotions to form. "Cat, I would like to apologize about how I treated you when we met."

Cat snorted. "You were probably right to treat me badly. Who needs a relationship—whether friendship or romantic?"

Gem frowned when he approached the steely older woman who had no affection for anything anymore. He laid a hand on her shoulder, noting that she was smaller than his hand. "We all need some type of relationship to get us through. My biggest sin is feeling absolutely nothing...romantically."

Cat scoffed, not buying his words. She barely touched the original flavored hot tea, because it wasn't her cup. She twisted in her seat to eye the young man. "That's not what Theo was calling you on when I appeared at The Clock. What's your issue, really, Gem?"

Gem squeezed her shoulder in a mindless act to distract them both. He heard grunting come from the apartment of Colette followed by a shriek, thud and exhausted sigh. "She cannot be that clumsy."

"You would be surprised." Cat huffed, not bothering to shrug off his comforting hand. She found much like the past that it was a meaningless gesture. She cut her eyes to the front door, coming full circle in her stool.

Colette flung open the front door with no need of a key. She was smoothing out the wrinkles in a gold dress that hugged her too tightly. Her makeup slacked since she had nothing to go with gold. She stumbled to walk in the gold, strapped high heels on her feet. "This is so not what I was going for!"

Gem gently stroked his chin as he eyed the blonde. He analyzed Colette from head to toe only for him to snap his fingers, turning her outfit blue with a tinge more color in her makeup. "Your favorite color, Queen C."

Cat's eyes flickered to Gem. "Queen C?"

"You'll learn more about us as the night wears on. Queen C loves to karaoke so this should prove to be a fruitful night, if nothing else." Gem casts Cat a wicked grin before winking at an embarrassed Colette.

"I can sing perfectly fine! Thank you!" Colette made sure to sign her frustration to Gem. She admired her red lips with an aqua blue eyeshadow that brought the blue shimmering dress, heels, and over the shoulder purse to life once more. She hardly asked anything of Gem Landry since the Air Shifter was a mere tenant, shocked by his attitude to help a sister out. She shared no blood with Gem, but thought of him as a younger brother with her eye on somebody to make her heart ache.

"She's in denial." Gem whispered to Cat who shuddered, hoping she would feel alright as she chose to remain quiet.

Cat didn't know what to say to Gem and Colette. She let them lead the way to **Meet at Midnight** which was a familiar place to her—somehow.

Seventeen

Meet at Midnight was silver and purple with plenty of magical beings on the dance floor or at the bar. Some magical beings were at a table or booth scattered about the stuffy, overcrowded club. It was a place that made The Swift Rose appear tame in comparison.

Cat couldn't breathe as she was sitting with Gem and Colette at the bar once the memories flooded her brain. She had been brought to **Meet at Midnight** when she turned eighteen by October who was tagging along with his friends. She didn't know just how sadistic his friends were, black mailing them once things took place in the back room that was recorded. She wouldn't ever be the same, forgiving none of them. It was a memory that she buried, allowing herself to believe that the last time she saw October was when she was sixteen.

"I shouldn't be here! This place drudges up bad memories!" Cat hisses to Gem and Colette.

Gem places a hand on her knee to get her to remain calm. His silver blue eyes hold assurance in them. "You'll stick with us, Cat. We'll make new memories together."

Colette giggled, having drank some more of her favorite raspberry flavored alcohol. She took a few shots, feeling the warm burn of eagerness take place. "It's time to sing!"

Gem nudged Cat, nodding to the stage past the bar in the back. "She's too buzzed to karaoke, but she's about to do it anyway! Watch."

Cat found a giddy change in the likes of Gem who was hanging all over her. She couldn't fathom why since he hardly ever drew to anyone. She sighed, following his deep blue eyes to the place Colette was already heading. "Are we sure she should be up on stage singing?"

Gem grinned, lightly poking the cheek of her face. He hadn't been drinking, compared to Colette and Cat.

Cat had taken a fancy to an ounce of vodka poured into the blue voltage mountain dew. She was glad they just called it, **Blue Voltage** or it would have been harder to remember. She tasted the mountain dew flavored alcohol at a slow pace, enjoying it.

Gem giggled into her shoulder. "N-no, but this isn't her first rodeo."

Cat sighed, allowing her shamrock green eyes to flit around the sea of magical beings. She became choked up once she caught sight of Hunter Coleman whose light green eyes were trained on Colette. She furrowed her eyebrows when Colette haphazardly winked directly at the man. "What in the—?"

Colette tapped the microphone before dedicating a few songs to Hunter. She began to sing while Gem interrupted Cat's question by pulling her up to her feet.

Cat lightly yelped as Gem swung her onto the dance floor causing her vision to dance with dots. She felt nausea creep into the pit of her stomach.

Gem began to sway with Cat pressing into him. His hand was warm on the small of her back as his friend pressed into her. He kept giggling which did more than startle her since she wasn't feeling the attraction.

Cat was swung around so many times by Gem that at one point, she went stumbling to the ground. She would have picked herself back up, but she wasn't sure that she cared to. The noise began to bother her head as did the flashing lights. "G-Gem?"

"Cat?" Gem croaked, stepping over the brunette as he wound up outside in the fresh air. He couldn't be in **Meet at Midnight** with Cat Devereaux causing him to flee the scene while she remained dizzy, scared, upset, and panicky.

Cat fumbled to drag her knees to her chest as she could have sworn she saw the familiar face of the one person she least expected to see. She couldn't look around for him with everything spinning her head out of control. Stray tears stained her cheeks as her jawline worked in irritation.

"Catarina?" His hand was light, barely visible on her knee. He had seen her with some other guy, really grinding his nerves. He saw the mess she was when she was forced to the dance floor by Gem Landry. He used his other hand to wipe a tear only to lift her chin so her eyes finally met his. "Breathe."

Cat was sure he was a figment of her imagination at that moment. She had plenty of panic attacks when she was young then he would turn up and ease them off. This time was no different, but she was one hundred percent that it was something she created to save herself the pain of the throbbing the dance floor gifted her head. "I cannot be seeing you!"

"I'm your imagination, right?" October asked, gently helping Cat to her feet. He could see the swirl of disbelief in her eyes. He placed a hand on the small of her back, leading her from the noise and flashing lights which seemed to calm her fast beating heart.

Cat scowled at the pain still surging in her head. "Yes. There's no way you'd be here in real time. Just no way."

"Why is that?" October asked, keeping close to Cat. He wanted her to know that she wasn't seeing or hearing things. He was actually with her, having been searching for answers in order to get to Tavi Devereaux. He was doing what he could to help Tasmin since Jade and Bellamy were getting on their nerves. He was even convinced by Tasmin to move into the black cherry cottage house just so he could avoid Jade.

"The real October just wouldn't show up unannounced or otherwise." Cat groaned, wiping away the rest of the tears the pain in her head had caused. She was thankful when the ache had started to wear off, allowing her a moment to think clearly even with the Blue Voltage.

October rubbed her back. "I show up wherever you go, it seems. When have you ever imagined me showing up where you turn up?"

Cat tilted her head to him once seated at the stool of the bar which was better than being on the dance floor. She was looking up at the grey hoodie clad ginger. "Are you trying to tell me you were actually present when I lost that basketball game in high school? I was playing just for fun, by the way."

"And, there's nothing wrong with that, but being short...doesn't help get it in the basket." October teased her, causing Cat to roll her eyes which was a mistake.

"I'm surprised you haven't crawled into bed with Jade. Isn't she the one you really want? How about my other sisters, sicko?!" Cat half growled, glaring at October. Her eyeballs burned when she rolled them into the back of head, returning the ache in her temples.

October shook his head, waiting for her full attention. "I didn't mean it. I have a stronger bond and connection with you, Catarina. I always have."

Cat sighed, choosing to lean into October. "Do you really mean that?"

October was about to confirm it for her when Colette's singing grew into sobbing. He was reluctant to tear his icy pale green eyes from hers. He gestured to the stage with the blonde. "Isn't your friend overdoing it?"

Colette sneezed into a tissue while a box of them sat next to her. She was a sentimental singer, blowing while sobbing into said tissue. She grabbed another tissue to clear up her tears. "I will always love you..."

October unplugged the microphone before Colette could destroy the classic song. He made a face when Colette grew confused about what happened. He shrugged while Cat weakly strode over to the blonde. "Time's up, blondie! Sorry."

"Are you taking me home, Red?" Colette smirks, walking over to October while sidestepping Cat. She ran a finger down his grey hoodie only to puke on the white sneakers of the ginger.

Cat grimaced as October froze, unsure of what to do. She placed a hand on the back of Colette, growing uneasy with the idea of touching another person. "Colette, we should get you home—to sleep off your drinks."

Irritation boiled in the blood of Colette. She could drink as much as she wanted without getting buzzed and drunk so quickly. Wiping a bit of vomit from her mouth, she stood to her height, shaking her head. "I'm not going anywhere! He poisoned my drink!"

October didn't move. He couldn't due to the vomit on his sneakers. He sighed. "Who poisoned your drink and why?"

"Hunter Coleman. He's my ex-husband!" Colette shrieked, throwing Cat's hand off of her. Her hazel blue eyes were wide with anger, nostrils flaring as she teleported in a glow of blue from her spot by the stage.

Cat tilted her head sideways with her shamrock green eyes on the place that Colette had previously stood. "Did she just say that Hunter is her ex-husband?"

October slowly nodded. "Yes, she very much did, Cat."

Cat frowned, flicking her eyes to the ginger. "Did she also just teleport?"

October began to nod his head in confirmation while Cat became fairly certain that he was a figment of her imagination. He saw the gleam of disbelief fill up her eyes once more. "I am not a figment of your imagination, Catarina. Sometimes, I break the mold and call you by your nickname. Sometimes."

Cat didn't see how Gem could have just ditched her at the club. "I wish I could teleport. Could you imagine playing basketball, teleporting in a swirl of gold from left to right to the basket?"

October grew amused by Cat. "That would be cheating at basketball, Cat."

"You could dribble while teleporting. It would be fun until that led to accidentally teleporting to space." Cat added, causing him to snort at her insane idea. She clasped her hands. "It could be basketball for magical beings such as me and anyone else who wants it—mostly just for fun."

"Cat, you get dizzy with lights and loud noise starts to cause your head to ache as if you had a bad tooth." October decided to remind her of her own issues.

"I'm still not convinced you aren't a part of my imagination as we speak." Cat said, watching something click in his brain.

"You're wearing the dress I bought you for Christmas." October spoke as his eyes slid to her body allowing his breath to hitch in the back of his throat. He was sure she wouldn't wear it since she promised not to. He didn't understand her logic as his own desire for the brunette returned tenfold. "You said you wouldn't ever wear it *unless*—"

Cat watched October cut his sentence short via his delayed realization. She wouldn't speak it into existence for him considering she wasn't young anymore. She saw his eyes widen and narrow as they returned to hers. "I had to be sure I was over you."

October raised an eyebrow as Cat became chilly in response towards him, shifting her gaze to the ground while her jaw set. He could tell by her body language that she didn't mean what she was voicing to him. "Is that why your date left you tonight?"

"I'm sorry, but even if I had a date that would not be your business." Cat groaned, heading towards the bar once more. She let her eyes scan the dance floor, finding no sight of Colette. Her eyes trailed up stairs to find Colette yelling at Hunter causing her to want to get to them as fast as possible.

"Cat!" October shouted, having rid his shoes of the vomit. He came into view just as the brunette vanished in a swirl of gold only to reappear next to Colette and Hunter.

Eighteen

Cat squeezed her eyes tight shut, stretching as warm, large arms engulfed her. She was in her safe place with the one person who made her feel at home. She felt the arms engulfing her grow tighter as she cuddled into the person's chest while lightly snoring. The more she realized she forgot the events of the club, the more awake she stirred. Her head still ached as she peeled open a shamrock green eye followed by her second one.

Her breasts were pressed into the face of the person she didn't expect to see holding her. She semi pulled back to frown at the position they were in, shaking her head. She remembered Colette informing her about the DNA results the blonde took on her behalf. She wasn't related to October by blood, but did that mean she wanted her body pressing into him? Other parts of her screamed for his touch, but her mind was sane enough to still fight against it.

Cat internally groaned, casting her eyes around the bedroom of her apartment. She would have recognized the powder blue walls with white trim anywhere. She was sure she had done nothing sinful with October, thinking of a way to squeeze out of his arms while not waking him up. She needed to remember what all happened the night prior. Has anything been learned on how to get into contact with Lucien Redmond?

Her mind was set on Tavi, wondering how her other sister was. She chewed on the thought when a chill coursed her body causing her to boost the thermostat. She proceeded further into the living room after gently closing her bedroom door. A visitor began a tap on the front door causing her eyebrows to weave into one. Who could be at her place so early?

Cat didn't bother to check the time as she peeled open the door, folding her arms to her bosom. She hadn't realized she was still in her dress from the previous night, thankful she was. "What do you want?"

"First off, I want to apologize for leaving you alone in **Meet at Midnight.** I'm usually not so reckless." Gem shakily voiced with an apology present in his blue eyes. Running a hand through his short, brown curls showcased that he was on edge. He had every right to be as he dug in his jacket pocket for something. "He left this for you."

Cat took a piece of paper with writing on it. "If you look within the puddle of water, outside your building, you'll find a door to the Underneath. Don't waste your breath choosing what to do. You have until it's washed away before you lose access to see her again."

"Lucien Redmond is quite the devil. Red hair, caramel skin and pale grey eyes. It's an ugly sight, no matter how good looking he is." Gem spoke, causing Cat to snort.

Did Cat even believe what she was reading to be true? What if it was false news? She gestured to the disheveled, broken down appearance of Gem. "Why do you look so rough, Gem? Wouldn't you have felt better giving me this while clean?"

Gem rolled his eyes, shaking his head. "It wasn't my idea to give you the knowledge on how to meet with the devil. In fact, you may want to talk to a particular blonde next door. She couldn't stop babbling about her brother all night with his evil, wicked, vile ways."

"Her brother?" Cat squeaked, not believing that Colette was related to the devil. Guilt surged to life in her heart which fluttered when she stepped back to peer over at her bedroom door. She didn't have to tell October where she was going nor did she want to.

"I can wait for him to wake up and explain to him where you went. Before you ask, I'm an Air Shifter, meant to guard your sister who threw a fit once she found out. We haven't spoken since she nearly ripped my ear from my head." Gem explained, once more gifting Cat with too much information.

Cat nodded in agreement, allowing Gem to enter her apartment who went directly to the kitchen. "Do me a favor, Gem, would you?"

Gem was already fumbling with the coffee pot. "Tea or coffee?"

"Coffee is what you want as early as this morning." Cat replied, gaining a half smile from Gem.

"Gets you going pretty good when the energy is required. You with your restoring energy power should be good though, Cat." Gem called to Cat who shrugged as he put on a pot of coffee.

Cat made sure she had her key in her jacket pocket before she closed the door to her apartment. Her eyebrow raised at the **A5** glued to Colette's front door. She twisted the doorknob, confused when she was able to open it so freely. She lightly knocked while calling to her friend. "Colette, it's me. Are you up?"

Colette groaned, tripping over a few things here and there. She wasn't prepared to deal with any visitors, given she barely recalled the events of the night before. All she did remember is Cat teleporting into the argument she maintained with Hunter. Her nostrils flared to life once the memory of the cheating, lying, dick sank in. "Y-yeah, just give me a minute."

Cat did as Colette commanded, less hostile on the other side of the door. She heard shuffling as the front door swung open to reveal the blonde. "I'd say you look like a mess, but you clean up nicer than Gem in the morning."

Colette's hair was styled, brushed with a strapless, heart shaped blue denim button up top, tucked into a set of blue denim shorts with dark blue leather boots that ran up to the tops of her knees. She placed a hand on her waist, aware of her grand style. "Thank you."

"Would you like to join me for some coffee?" Cat asked, causing Colette to scowl.

Colette swung open the door to her apartment, ushering Cat into her humble abode. Her apartment looked the exact same as Cat's except hers was in a darker shade of blue with more sound proofing. She led the way to the kitchen, using a finger to gesture for Cat to join her. "I'll make us a cuppa."

Cat scoffed. "If it's not peppermint and hot then no thank you."

Colette smiled, creating two cups in thin air. She handed a red and white one to Cat, using her magic for just about everything. "It might just be peppermint flavored and hot."

Cat sipped from the mug, feeling her insides warm up. The peppermint tea made her taste buds dance allowing a smile to break the mold. She cheered with Colette by lightly touching their mugs to one another. "Now, that's what I call peppermint tea."

"So, what's up? Gem came to see you which meant he told you something I said or did while buzzed." Colette informed Cat who was happy that she was okay. She had been aware of her ex-husband admitting to poisoning them both for his vengeance nor was she about to deal with it.

"Lucien Redmond." Cat spoke the name, gently sitting at a stool in the kitchen.

Colette leaned on the counter, making sure her cuppa was up to her standards. She took a few sips before cutting her hazel blue eyes to Cat. "Lucien Redmond is my brother. What of it?"

"There's a puddle outside that acts as a portal to the Underneath?" Cat fishes for the information whereas Colette is happy to answer her. She would have assumed that Colette was equally as evil as her brother.

"Yes, there is. You can step through to visit your dear old sister and see how things are." Colette informs Cat, nodding to her outfit. "Are you sure you want an audience with the devil and his betrothed wearing last night's outfit?"

Cat drank more of the peppermint tea feeling her energy become restored for the day. She raised an eyebrow as more questions presented themselves to her brain. "Will your brother kill me? How can you be so open with talking about him?"

"Contrary to what you were told, Catarina, there is no evil in the Underneath or roaming the Earth unless you count the bad seeds that opt to go rogue. I can be wicked or a trickster, but killing a man is another ball game." Colette darkly chuckles as astonishment slams into Cat.

"What about Sage Landry?" Cat did a double take as Colette scoffed.

"Sage Landry was nothing more than a clone of Gem Landry, ripped from the seams of a hair, built in the mirror image of that poor boy. Lucien had nothing to do with his creation—that would be Hunter's doing." Colette speaks, rolling her hazel blue eyes at the memory of her ex.

Cat finishes her tea, pointing to the mug. "What do you want me to do with this?"

Colette softly smiles as she touches a finger to the mug. She caused it to become one with thin air, vanishing as she cuts her eyes to the dazed features of Cat. "You should get ready for your meeting with the devil, should you not?"

Cat was about to walk out of Colette's door when the blonde coughed to gather her attention. "What? Did I misstep?"

"Oh, no. You can teleport in a swirl of gold, Catarina. You did so at the club last night to get in between the argument I had with Hunter." Colette informs Cat who is starting to remember more of the night.

Cat had teleported to them, confused about how she got home; held together by October. She chewed on her bottom lip, believing more and more in her powers. A swirl of gold encompasses her body, teleporting her to her bathroom connected to her bedroom. She hears the groggy voice of October conversing with Gem. She peels open her bathroom door, thankful October had shut the bedroom upon leaving.

She scurried around her bedroom, plucking up an outfit for the day before returning to the bathroom. She took a nice, hot shower only to dry off, brush her teeth only to get changed. She wore a vibrant red tank top tucked into a black skirt, stockings and black ankle boots. A frown placated her features at the outfit since it had been another gift from Jade. She returned to Colette in a swirl of gold who cracked a grin at how fast the Faerie was getting a hang of her power.

"I can't believe, you're the Faerie of the Sun and your older sister is the Faerie of the Moon. You two have the coolest gift known to man." Colette confessed in a giddy squeal to Cat who hadn't known much about herself.

Cat nodded to her outfit. "Is this alright to meet the devil in?"

"No, Lucien prefers it hotter, but it'll have to do or you'll be wasting time." Colette yawned, causing her fingernails to become a frosty blue, elongated to show more of her own fashion sense. She enjoyed being a woman. A realization occurred to her. "You seem to be red while I'm blue."

Cat had noticed their red and blue schemes of a pattern between them. She was best suited for red and black even when she tried to move away from the color. She shrugged. "That rhymed."

Colette chuckled. "Yep. You should be good."

"How do I get back if the puddle is gone?" Cat asks a daft question as Colette sports a smirk.

"How do you think, Cat?" Colette sipped on some more of her cuppa. She was going to take her time since she had all morning while her newly made friend met with the devil. She was sure her brother would approve of her friendship with Cat. She yawned as she made sure to voice what Cat was slow to process. "Use your teleportation to leave the Underneath if the portal is closed."

Nineteen

Fire cackling could be heard once Cat stepped into the Underneath. Red and dusted cavern walls were on either side as she walked down a matching flight of stairs. She saw a river of flaming lava causing confusion to seep into her. Hadn't somebody told her that the flames would be blue in the Underneath? Shaking her head, she wound up in what appeared to be a homey space.

A white sofa with a television screen was in an open space of a small, boring kitchen and dining room. It wasn't the best housing assortment while Tavi Devereaux scuttled about clearing cobwebs.

"Octavia?" Cat whispered into the atmosphere causing her sister to freeze in place.

Tavi shook her head of healthy, lengthy, charcoal brown hair. Her navy green eyes shone with brightness as her belly had grown bigger. She would deliver the triplets any day which meant she needed to be on the surface of Earth. She was tight-lipped in her delusion. "I must be hearing things."

Cat raised her hands, clasping them together as loudly as possible. She saw her sister in a black gown tense once more. She waited for Tavi to realize she was indeed not alone. "TAVI!"

The roar of her second older sister made Tavi rethink her so-called delusions. She threw the duster down, eagerly turning to find Cat Devereaux amongst her company. "CAT!"

Cat's legs wobbled as the room shook with the loudness of their yelling. She became uneasy, inhaling sharply. "You haven't had them yet?"

"Nope. Haven't been wed either." Tavi rushed over, gripping the wrists of Cat.

Cat briefly embraced Tavi, aware a squeeze too tight may not be healthy for the mother. She cut her eyes around, searching for the devil who had her trapped. "Where is Lucien Redmond?"

"Lucien is out on business, but he should be back at any given minute." Tavi said, tugging her sister over to the sofa. She showed Cat the silver diamond ring on her left middle finger. "He's marrying me."

"Why? Wouldn't that do you more harm than good?" Cat questioned, confused about who Lucien Redmond was exactly. She furrowed her eyebrows. "He's the devil."

"Not like you're thinking. He treats me right—like a queen." Tavi informs Cat with a grin so wide that her sister believed every word of it. She wasn't lying either as she sighed. "This is where I belong. He owns my heart."

Cat's gaze went from the feet of Tavi to her head, unable to detect any falseness stemming from her sister. She shrugged. "As long as you're happy. Has Taz made her way to you?"

"No, and as far as I know, Jade has flipped a lid." Tavi hissed, squeezing the wrist of Cat harder than she should.

Cat tugged her grip from Tavi, leaning out of her sister's orbit. She glanced around the Underneath once more, frowning at the irritation of it all. "How can you live like this?"

"I just can, Cat. You should try being happy for a change." Tavi muttered, knowing her sister needed to find something for herself. She was with Lucien Redmond—nothing would change that. She was about to be wed to the devil in order to spare her triplets a life without their father.

"Hunter Coleman kept you locked away in a house for years. You believe this is what you want, because of those years?" Cat asked her sister, catching the panic surface in the navy green eyes of Tavi. She pressed the back of her hand to the forehead of a profusely sweating Tavi Devereaux.

Tavi shook her head. "I don't think he'll like you, Cat. You should leave before he returns."

Cat set her jaw, stubborn as could be. Seeing how her sister was acting made her want to have a word with the devil even more. She rolled her shamrock green eyes at Tavi. "I'm staying to have a word with the devil on your behalf."

"He's not the devil!" Tavi insisted, standing up to flee the scene. She hurried to the bedroom she slept, separate from Lucien Redmond who promised to seal the deal after they tied the knot. She felt even more trapped than with Hunter.

Cat ground her teeth just as the chuckle of Lucien Redmond caught her off guard. She lifted an eyebrow, turning to a broad shouldered, caramel complected, ginger haired man. "Oof, you're definitely a sight for sore eyes!"

"Thank you, Cat." Lucien Redmond chuckled with his pale grey eyes lingering on her body. He was in a dark grey, polo shirt with the collar pressed down. He wore dark blue jeans and dark grey sneakers to complete his attire. His hair was short, messy, and held a smidge of curls. "You seem to be struggling with letting go of your hold on Tavi. You should be able to since you fled the ranch house."

"How do you know what I do?" Cat is aggravated when the question falls from her lips. She catches him sigh as he shakes his head due to her daftness. "Are you some devilish spy?"

"I'm not a spy, Cat. On occasion, I check in with the family of my beloved, my betrothed." Lucien says, cracking a grinch-like grin.

"It doesn't matter. Listen to me, Lucien, Tavi has been locked up for ages thanks to Hunter Coleman. If you're so good, let alone decent, why are you trying to clip her wings further?" Cat rattled off as Lucien grimaced.

Lucien hadn't realized the effects of the damage Hunter did to Tavi. He rubbed his chin as something occurred to him. He should have started with the information that would put Cat at ease. "Once I marry Tavi and her triplets enter the world, she can come and go as she pleases. My plan wasn't to hold her hostage, but to help ensure her safety, especially from the likes of Coleman."

Cat shoved down the sense of relief trying to clutch her heart. She scoffed. "Can you give me proof or are you so wicked that you can't even be bothered?"

"You'll receive your proof once the wedding is over and done with as well as her pregnancy." Lucien said, taking a seat on the sofa as something slides into his brain. "Would you like a test of wills, Catarina?"

Cat stood up, brushing off the outfit she wore. She wasn't sure she liked where Lucien was going with the gleam of mischief surfacing in his pale grey eyes. "I've been tested too many times since returning to Silver Hart. How many more tests of wills do I have to go through?"

"There's a place where the magic of Silver Hart is stored. You and your sister are the only ones who should know about it since your magic comes from the sun and hers the moon. It's a place of imagination..." Lucien trailed off, doing what he could to intrigue her.

Cat tilted her head at Lucien. She bit her bottom lip. She had to ask herself if she wanted any more tests. She thought over the question, gaining an eye roll from Lucien? "What is this place? Why should I keep testing myself?"

"You shouldn't keep testing yourself, Cat." Lucien disagreed as a smirk cracked his lips. He wiggled his eyebrows at her. "The Silver Hollow is where you'll fully learn more about yourself and your magic. It's not a test for you, Cat, but it's a test for you and your partner. You see? The Silver Hollow splits romantic ties, and romantic notions—"

"Leaving one with apathy and no room to feel?" Cat squeaked as a newfound panic set into her heart. She began to pace in front of the devil. She didn't like the sound of the suggestion as she shook her head.

"Catarina, haven't you been through enough emotion to last you a lifetime? Aren't you done feeling hurt and torment for the one person who has cost you everything?" Lucien begged to differ when asking her such personal, hostile questions. He wasn't asking for himself, but for the greater good.

Cat fumbled with the reality of the situation. She stopped pacing in front of the devil, facing him. Her bottom lip turned down into a pout. "October isn't the issue. He was, but then..."

"The truth came to fruition and you couldn't stand to live without him, yeah?" Lucien quipped, gaining a slow, but gentle nod of the head from the woman. He proceeds to nonchalantly shrug until it clicks in his head. "Are you absolutely sure you want to be wrapped in red for the rest of your life? You're only twenty nine with more life left to live—he's holding you back."

Cat considered the words of Lucien very carefully. She couldn't tell anyone how to live like they couldn't tell her how to live. She chews on her bottom lip, thinking about the fire she had with October. She hated how one minute she could jump him then the next she wanted to never see him again. She had to do something for herself for a change, not yearning to risk being with October Winston after all their years of turmoil. She sighed. "You do have a point there."

"Exactly, Miss Independent. October Winston will always burn a soft spot in your heart, but do you want to settle for him? You've been on and off, but do you truly love him or did that affection fade once the truth surfaced?" Lucien was asking smart questions that Cat had the answers to.

For the longest time, Cat had convinced herself that she had been in love with October. For a brief period, that affection did exist, but over the years she changed. Her affection for the ginger began to wane, slowly but surely which was a part of the reason her attitude towards him had shifted. Could she love him and be her own, strong woman? Laughing at the idea, she came to a quick decision, pointing to Lucien. "How do I leave The Silver Hollow?"

"You don't just willingly leave, Cat." Lucien explained, causing him to grimace. He did know how she could leave though as he cleared his throat. "You have to wait for The Silver Hollow to pardon you—if you don't things could get bad. It's overflowing with magic so do what you can, not to upset it."

"Could I teleport out of there?" Cat asked as Lucien grinned, snapping his fingers before pointing at her. She must have been on a roll.

"You got it, Cat. I'm aware that you want to open a basketball game for magical beings with the idea of teleporting." Lucien muttered, causing a blush of embarrassment to flicker to life on her cheeks.

Cat beamed. "How d-did you know?"

"I will check in with you for the sake of Tavi. Not all the time, but every once in a grey flicker, I'll find intriguing conversations. The Sun Realm is where you can hold your basketball games." Lucien said, offering up a solution to an idea.

Cat scoffed, folding her arms to her bosom. "The Sun Realm?"

"There's a Sun Realm, Moon Realm, Air Realm, Fire Realm, Earth Realm and Water Realm." Lucien snorts in reply to Cat. He thought with her being a Faerie that the differing realms would have been obvious. "Sadly, every single one of them aside from the Sun, Moon and Earth Realm are extinct which is why you have air, fire and water planted on Earth."

Cat would have to learn more history about herself if she wanted to be knowledgeable about her world. She sighed, nodding her head in agreement. "I can learn about the realms later…"

Lucien held up a finger only for the man to clear his throat. "I do hope you know what you're doing, Catarina. Once you split your romance—there's no going back. You won't fall in love ever again."

Cat fumbled for the words in her brain, but she came up with a blank space. She couldn't afford to love him anymore. "I'm ready."

Twenty

The Silver Hollow turned out to be an isolated forest drenched in silver treetops and a lake with a pier. It was hauntingly beautiful, enough to take someone's breath away. It stole the breath from Cat Devereaux who placed a hand over her heart as her beat grew to change. A sharp sting started within before nothing washed over Cat. She didn't love him, she didn't love anyone.

A frown placated her dark pink lips, pursing them as her shamrock green eyes took in the scenery with pitch black skies that excluded the stars. An eyebrow rose once she realized The Silver Hollow was indeed hollow just as the namesake it held. She blew a raspberry as light giggles erupted all around her, making her head hurt.

"From here on out, you will reign as the Silver Queen." A feminine giggle escaped a small, silver fairy floating into Cat's view. She was about as small as a dragonfly with a giggle that could be taken to a chalkboard.

"The Silver Queen? I'm the Faerie of the Sun!" Cat hissed in utter confusion.

"Yes, when you are on Earth, but when you visit The Silver Hollow—you are our queen." The fairy grinned as she held a key out towards Cat.

Cat extended a flat palm towards the fairy which wasn't the same as her kind of Faerie. "Um...what shall I call you?"

"Ariana." The fairy silkily replied with a glazed over look surfacing in her silver eyes. She laughed as an afterthought seemed to occur to her. "You won't need a King. The Silver Queen hardly does. What can we do for you today, amour?"

Cat felt the lightness of the key drop into her palm at the same time of her response to the small being. "I am in a test of wills."

"A test you shall have." Ariana giggled, vanishing into the darkness.

Cat grew nauseous as her vision dotted once a pop sounded next to her. Her outfit had changed in The Silver Hollow which spit her out in the streets of downtown Silver Hart. She spun around, finding everything except herself had become normal. "What the...?"

"Check your pocket!" The hiss of Ariana infiltrated her head.

Cat dug into a pair of black shorts with a silver, sparkly vest over a gray tee shirt. Her shoes remained as her black ankle boots which caused her to snort. She found advice written on a slither of silver paper in black and white ink. "There is no other test than your emotionless state." Her tongue felt heavy as she opted to remember who she was, frowning upon touching her singed, thick, brown curls.

Her hair had been cut to frame her cheeks with silver highlights embedded at the bottom of dark brown curls. She shook her head, starting in the direction of Air Loft since her surroundings had begun to readjust. Something was off as she found no sign of Colette Redmond at the desk of the lobby. She strode to the right when she walked into the hall which would take her to their apartments. She lightly knocked on the door of Colette's apartment.

"Ooh." Colette beamed with excitement upon seeing Cat Devereaux. She frowned as she noticed the change in her friend. She shook her head as she spoke before the brunette with silver in her hair could open her mouth. "You must have been in The Silver Hollow for the past year."

Shock attempted to take the place of Cat's numbness, but failed to gain the upper hand. Her brain felt as if it had been in a fog so her disappearance for over a year made sense. "How could you tell?"

"There's silver in your hair. When the Silver Hollow barely keeps you, silver doesn't show up in your hair. You've been gone for a year—everybody has moved on." Colette quipped, having ripped the heart from Hunter Coleman's chest.

Cat lifted an eyebrow. "What about Taz and Jade?"

"Jade got married and moved with her husband, Bellamy, down south to Georgia. Don't you remember her telling you this? I went to the wedding and that little wench was so rude." Colette irritably announced, rolling her hazel blue eyes.

Cat wondered about the one person who always ruined her progress. "What about October Winston?"

"He returned to the ranch so Tasmin wouldn't be by herself." Colette replied as she nonchalantly shrugged.

Cat chewed on the idea of popping in to visit her sister, but if she didn't then how would she know if she truly no longer had emotion for October? She sighed, ready to teleport to Tasmin when Colette cleared her throat. "Did you get your revenge on Hunter?"

Colette beamed from ear to ear, eagerly nodding her head in agreement. "He's a dead, P.O.S."

Cat fumbled for 'a congratulations' since she found killing the shadow a bit too much. The blood wasn't on her hands, so, why should she give a fudge? Shaking it off, she shot Colette a half smile. "No romance for you either then?"

"Not until the right one walks through the door." Colette giggled, winking as Cat rolled her shamrock green eyes to the roof of the apartment complex.

Cat backed up while Colette gently closed the front door to her apartment. Without a second thought, she teleported to the Devereaux Ranch in a swirl of gold. She was on the front porch, casting her eyes about the place, not coming across much change. Lifting her hand to knock on the front door, Tasmin was already peeling it open. "Taz?"

"Cat." Tasmin spoke her name with some ice in her tone. She was glad to see that her middle sister was okay, having been completely ghosted by Tavi from the year prior. She heard no more word from Jade either which put a strain on her heart. "Why don't you come in for tea?"

Cat strode through the front door, frowning when she didn't catch sight of October. "What happened to Winston?"

Tasmin snorted, finally taking in the silver in the brown hair of Cat. She noticed everything about her sister had changed. She shouldn't even be shocked since Cat hadn't spoken to her in a good year. "The Silver Hollow. Why am I not surprised?"

Cat snorts, allowing her eyebrows to weave together. She followed the saddened glance of Tasmin to her change in appearance as they ended up in the living room. "Taz, it was for the best. I would have been stuck pining away for October—on and off."

"You don't have to worry about wanting October. He's gone. He left about a month after you fled the Earth." Tasmin spoke, carrying in a tray of tea after going to retrieve it from the kitchen, pouring them both some. She wiped her hands down the front of her brown skirt as she handed Cat a cup. She then sat on the sofa, waiting for Cat to do the same.

"I thought Winston returned to keep you company since you'd be in this big ole' house alone. Shouldn't you be afraid of somebody breaking in?" Cat posed a good question while Tasmin snorted. She set her cup on the coffee table, not craving food or any beverage.

Tasmin grimaced while taking in the demeanor and behavior of her sister. She should have known that once Tavi spoke Cat's disappearance into the Silver Hollow into existence; an emotionless sister is what they'd get. "You can't be worried about me since The Silver Hollow stripped you of your romantic emotions including your natural ones. You won't have any basic instincts either. I hope you realize what you've done."

Cat scoffed, rolling her shamrock green eyes. She begged to differ, feeling as good as she assumed she would feel. "I can't speak for you or anyone else, but this is the best I've ever been. If I had what they stripped me of then like I said, I'd be pining away for someone just like every other ignorant woman."

Tasmin couldn't hide the hurt or annoyance she began to feel towards her daft sister. "Catarina, you don't mean that."

"I say what I mean and I do what I mean. Nothing more, nothing less. I'm going to be fresh for as long as I live." Cat said, biting into the rage clouding her judgement where Tasmin was concerned. She didn't want her sister to attempt to ruin a good thing for her.

"October went to work for a soda company—a specific brand of soda." Tasmin changed the subject, wanting to slap Cat, but she held her temper in check.

Cat sighed, nonchalantly shrugging. "He isn't my problem anymore."

"October still very much loves you." Tasmin snorted, unsure as to why since her sister had changed. She didn't find the change for the better—no one could convince her otherwise either.

Cat blew out a breath, shrugging. "And?"

"I don't care if you have no emotion, Cat. I care that October could be dead." Tasmin hissed, dropping her tea mug. She winced when it clattered, shattering to the ground. She didn't care since she had been concerned about the gingers well-being for over a few months. She had been promised by October that he would write and call to ensure that he was okay.

"October is good at making promises that he prefers to break." Cat gently informed Tasmin, feeling a shred of humanity tug at her heart. If she helped to locate October then maybe, she could go back to her corner of a fresh life.

Tasmin quirked an eyebrow at Cat. "He always checks in with us. Always."

"Fine. What's the name of this soda company?" Cat quips, yawning as Tasmin told her. Her shamrock green eyes widened in astonishment by the name. "That name is for a particular soda, not a brand for a company of that soda."

"Do you think we should check it out?" Tasmin squeaked with worry present on her face. She searched the eyes of Cat who wanted anything, but to check up on October.

Cat took Tasmin's hand before they disappeared in a swirl of gold. She took them to the outside of a white brick building—on the other side of Silver Hart. She saw it had no name written on the wall as she wandered over to a rusted, metal door. "There's no question about checking it out, Taz."

Tasmin held hope that Cat's emotions could be restored. She knew that if Cat didn't get her emotions back as quickly as she had lost them, they would have lost the Faerie of the Sun. "It's awfully dark and stale in here."

Cat ignored Tasmin, striding into said darkness to find it was a factory with cobwebs, dust, and age old objects—unsold and unboxed with boxes. She coughed, walking as light as a feather until she stumbled across a closed eye, pale faced familiar ginger who was buried under old boxes of toys and gadgets. She crouched down, trying not to cough as she touched a hand to his face while fearing the worst. "Tober?"

October Winston had been drained to the point that his lips were dried and cracked. He was on the cusp of death, believing he had died. He was told by the owner that he was meant to be an ingredient in their ginger ale. His chest rose and fell trying to find his voice while fighting to open his icy green eyes. "C-Cat?"

Sorrow infiltrated Cat's body as warmth engulfed her. Gold light poured from her into October restoring his life force and healing him. She didn't get a chance to speak, aware that she had failed the test of The Silver Hollow and herself. "Oct—"

October kissed Cat in a short, feverish kiss that could have been longer if not for the clearing of Tasmin's throat. His eyebrows met his hairline when his icy pale green eyes locked on hers. "I love you, Cat."

Cat shattered, feeling her heart hammer in her chest. A brief midnight haze had swamped her body only for her sorrow to be eradicated. She was going to burn in fire. "Taz?"

Tasmin approached the two after interrupting the kiss. She had been disgusted by the sight. "How about we get you home?"

Cat and Tasmin helped October up who removed himself from both women.

October was confused about Cat's distance from him. He saw the silver in her hair which seemed to be vanishing, returning her brown ends to their natural state. "Cat—"

"I will meet you two later. I have to readjust to my living space." Cat said, vanishing from October and Tasmin in a swirl of gold. She couldn't be in the same space as October—not wanting to be his. She had phantom tears spark to life in her eyes as the floodgates of emotion had reopened.

About the Author

Madaline Clifton

Madaline Clifton was born on a Spring day in March. She's always had a creative mind ever since she was young. She's been writing for as long as she can remember, grateful for those along the way. Her favorite genre to write is her own version of fantasy and paranormal with a variety of blends. She's into music, books, television shows, some movies along with her loner status plus she adores cats and nature.

9 789367 956755